Welcome to Suite 4B!

Gone to the stables

Jina

Shh!! Studying—
please do not disturb!

Mary Beth

<u>GO AWAY!!!</u>

Andie

Hey, guys!
Meet me downstairs in the
common room. Bring popcorn!

Lauren

Join Andie, Jina, Mary Beth, and Lauren for more fun at the Riding Academy!

Mary Beth shivered in the cool night breeze as she and Tommy walked their horses along the dark trail.

Suddenly, the wind whipped through the trees, sending a plastic-bag ghost flying from a limb. The ghost hit Lukas on the flank, startling Tommy's already-nervous horse.

He reared sharply, throwing Tommy backward. The reins flew from Tommy's hands. He grabbed for the pommel as Lukas wheeled around, crashing into Dan's side.

Mary Beth was jolted forward.

"Lukas, whoa!" Tommy commanded.

Head high, nostrils flared, Lukas paused just long enough for Mary Beth to bend down and snatch up the reins. Suddenly, the gray bolted forward, his instinct telling him to run.

Desperately, Mary Beth held on tight, willing her own horse to stand firm…

MARY BETH'S HAUNTED RIDE

by Alison Hart

BULLSEYE BOOKS

Random House ⌂ New York

"He's coming! He's coming!" Mary Beth Finney shouted as she danced into suite 4B, waving a piece of paper. She twirled in a circle, her auburn hair flying behind her.

"Who's coming?" Lauren Remick, one of her roommates, asked. She was sitting on the edge of her bed, pulling on her left riding boot.

Mary Beth fell backward on the bed in a swoon. "*Brad!* I just got a letter from him."

Lauren glanced up and grinned. Her long blond braid dangled over her shoulder. "Brad's coming for Parents' Weekend? That's so cool!"

Mary Beth propped herself up on her elbows, her green eyes sparkling. "In two weeks, my whole family's driving to Foxhall. Brad said he'd have to check with his mom and dad, but if it was okay with them, he's dying to come, too."

1

Lauren's mouth dropped open in surprise. "He's *dying* to come? Wow."

"Well—" Mary Beth's freckled cheeks reddened. "He didn't actually say *dying*."

Standing up, Lauren pounded her left boot heel against the tile floor. "Well, you'll be the only sixth-grader who has a date for Parents' Weekend. Too bad he can't come this weekend, for the big Halloween dance."

Mary Beth, Lauren, and their two roommates, Andie Perez and Jina Williams, were all students at Foxhall Academy, a private boarding school in Maryland. This weekend, Foxhall had invited the boys from the Manchester School for Halloween activities.

"Oh, Brad doesn't like to dance," Mary Beth said quickly. Then she stared at Lauren, who continued to stomp on the floor. "What are you doing?" Mary Beth was a beginning rider, and she was always asking questions.

"Trying to get this stupid boot on," Lauren explained. "You'd better get ready for your riding lesson, too, or you'll be late."

Reluctantly, Mary Beth sat up. "I'm so excited about Brad, I won't be able to concentrate." Then she sighed, remembering yesterday's riding lesson. Dan, her assigned school horse, had poked along, ignoring her squeezes and clucks. Today the muscles on the inside of her thighs were so sore from trying to get him to move that she was walking bowlegged. "Dan was so awful yesterday," she told Lauren.

"I thought you and Dan were getting along great," Lauren said.

"Oh, we are—I guess. At least I don't have to worry about him bucking me off."

Jumping off the bed, Mary Beth began to hunt for her riding helmet. Since four girls shared the suite, it was always impossible to find things. Finally, she spotted the helmet lying on a stack of jeans on the top shelf of the wardrobe. When she pulled it from the shelf, the pants tumbled to the floor.

"Whose pants are these, anyway?" Mary Beth grumbled as she bent to pick them up.

"Well, they were folded neatly, so they have to be Jina's. They sure can't be Andie's," Lauren said, glancing at Andie's bed by the window. A blanket had been hastily pulled up over the pillow, and dirty underwear was piled in the middle.

Mary Beth stuffed the jeans back onto the shelf. "Where are those two, anyway?"

"Andie went up to the stables already," Lauren said. "Dorothy is helping her bridle and saddle Magic. It's the first time in three weeks, so Andie is really excited."

Mr. Magic, the handsome but wild Thoroughbred Andie leased from the school, had recently had an operation on his eye.

"Is she going to ride him?" Mary Beth asked.

Lauren zipped a windbreaker over her sweatshirt. "Not yet. Oh, and Jina's gone to Middlefield with Todd to see Applejacks."

Todd Jenkins was Jina's trainer. Since her horse, Superstar, was lame, Todd had convinced Jina to show Applejacks. He was a pony owned by a client at the prestigious Middlefield Stables where Jina took private riding lessons.

"Are you coming?" Lauren waited impatiently in the doorway.

Mary Beth waved her away. "I'll catch up."

"Okay." Lauren wiggled her fingers in a good-bye and clomped noisily down the hall. Mary Beth kicked off her tennis shoes and pulled her paddock boots from under her bed.

As she laced up the boots, she thought about Brad.

They were just friends, really. The two of

4

them had been next-door neighbors for years, so they'd spent a lot of time hanging around together. It would be neat to see Brad over Parents' Weekend, but it wouldn't be a *date*.

So why was she making such a big deal out of this and telling her roommates that Brad was her boyfriend?

Unfolding the letter, Mary Beth read it for the fourth time.

Dear Mary Beth,
 You sure aren't missing much here at Cedarville Elementary. Mrs. Henderson's chin hairs are even longer. Danny swears he's going to shave them. Emily Zentz sits in front of me. Janie sits behind me. They're always passing notes across my desk. I used to read them, but they write such dumb stuff, I don't bother anymore.
 I'll ask my mom and dad about coming for Parents' Weekend. It sounds like fun. See you then.
                                   Brad

Last year, Janie had been her best friend. Was Janie best friends with Emily now?

Mary Beth felt a sudden pang of homesickness. She had wanted to go to Foxhall Academy because it had such a super math and science program. Still, she missed everybody back in Cedarville.

Except Emily Zentz.

Mary Beth remembered Emily from fifth grade. She laughed like a hyena. Still, she had long, brown hair that actually *bounced,* and the boys loved to chase her on the playground.

Hastily, Mary Beth pulled her jacket from the back of the chair, folded up the letter, and stuck it in a pocket.

Best friends, passing notes, chasing boys— that was all baby stuff, she told herself. She was at Foxhall Academy now, and it was time for her riding lesson. She'd just have to think about Brad and Janie and Emily later.

"Don't you dare take a bite of grass!" Mary Beth warned Dan as the group of beginning riders rode their horses down the drive to the outdoor ring. As always, Dangerous Dan, a huge part-draft horse, meandered toward the grassy edge. Mary Beth dug her right heel into his side, trying to force him over. Ignoring her, he stuck out his nose, pulling the reins through her fingers, and snatched a bite of grass.

"Dan!" Mary Beth yelled as she yanked on the reins. "Get your big, fat head up."

"Don't let him eat, Mary Beth!" Dorothy, the stable manager, hollered over her shoulder. Turning, she put her hands on her wide hips and frowned at Mary Beth. She wore grass-stained jeans and a T-shirt that said, A HORSE IS TO RIDE (AND LOVE).

"I'm trying not to," Mary Beth shouted back. She gave Dan a kick, but he didn't budge.

Dorothy came over and nudged the horse's nose with her foot. "Stop eating, you clod," she scolded.

Dan's head popped up, and the reins flew everywhere. Exasperated, Mary Beth gritted her teeth as she gathered them up.

"Reins between the little finger and third finger," Mary Beth recited to herself, making sure she was holding them correctly. "The thumb goes on top."

Most of the other riders in Foxhall's riding program were already warming up their horses in the outdoor rings. Lauren and Whisper, her assigned horse, were cantering gracefully in a small circle around Katherine Parks, the dressage instructor. Last Saturday, Lauren had won a fifth place in a local dressage competition.

"Ready, Mary Beth?" Dorothy asked impatiently.

Heidi Olsen and Shandra Thomas, two other beginning riders, had stopped, too. They were turned in their saddles, watching Mary Beth fix her reins.

Mary Beth flushed. Why was she always the one who had trouble?

"Ready," she said.

Dorothy walked beside Dan until he and Mary Beth reached the ring. At least Dan wouldn't try to eat there. The ring was covered with tanbark. Now Mary Beth just had to worry about getting her horse to pay attention.

When she'd first been assigned Dangerous Dan, she'd been relieved to find out his name was just a joke. He was, as Dorothy put it, dead quiet. But after a month and a half of dealing with a horse like Dan, Mary Beth knew how hard it was to get "dead quiet" moving.

"Hey, Finney!" a loud voice called.

Mary Beth snapped around as Andie Perez strode up to Dan and patted him soundly on his chestnut neck. Andie had thick, wavy hair that she'd pulled back in a scrunchie. Still, wild strands blew everywhere in the crisp October breeze.

"What are you doing in the ring?" Mary Beth asked.

Andie grinned. "I finished with Magic early, so Caufield told me to help Dorothy with you baby riders."

"Here, Mary Beth," Dorothy said, walking up to them. She carried a riding whip. "We're going to try this on Dan."

Mary Beth's brows shot up. "You want me to *hit* him with that?"

Andie smothered a laugh.

"Not exactly," Dorothy said. "You should just have to tap him once or twice."

"Oh." Mary Beth gingerly took the whip.

Dorothy showed her how to hold it. "Carry it in your inside hand. That means, if you're circling to the right, you hold it in your right hand. When you squeeze your legs against Dan's side to ask for a walk or a trot, he should respond. If he doesn't, grab the reins with your outside hand. Then reach down and tap him behind your leg with the whip at the same time you give the aid again."

"Ugh." Mary Beth frowned. "I'll never remember all that."

"Don't worry, Andie will help you. Try it once or twice when you ask Dan to move from the halt to the walk."

Dorothy left to adjust Heidi's girth. Heidi had been riding since the beginning of school, too. But she was ready to canter by now.

"If I were you, I'd give Dan a good whack," Andie said. "He's half asleep."

"No way." Mary Beth shook her head. "I don't want to hurt him."

Andie snorted. "Hurt this big moose? You've got to show him who's boss."

"I guess," Mary Beth said, trying not to sound so uncertain. "I *am* pretty sick of sore muscles." She squared herself in the saddle, then took a deep breath. "Okay, here goes." Squeezing her calves hard against Dan's sides, she asked him to walk. He switched his tail and flapped his lips sleepily.

"See? He's ignoring you, Finney." Andie looked sternly at Mary Beth. "This time when you give him the aid and he doesn't walk, smack him."

Mary Beth grimaced. "Really?"

Andie nodded. "Be tough."

"Okay." Maybe Andie was right. Mary Beth was tired of being the worst rider at Foxhall, especially when all her roommates were so good. It was time to prove she could at least get her horse to obey.

Again, Mary Beth squeezed her legs hard against Dan's sides. When he didn't move, she took both reins in her left hand. Then she reached back and whacked him hard on the right side.

With a startled snort, Dan lurched forward. Mary Beth snapped backward so hard her arms flew in the air and she lost her reins. Dan took off, trotting briskly to the railing. Mary Beth was tossed up and down as if she were on a trampoline. She bounced hard in the saddle, her feet jiggling uselessly in the stirrups.

Panicking, Mary Beth clutched Dan's mane, but she could feel herself sliding down the horse's left side.

Her worst nightmare was about to happen. She was going to fall!

"Whoa!" Mary Beth croaked as Dan trotted toward the group of riders cantering at the other end of the ring.

"Emergency dismount!" Dorothy hollered.

The stable manager's shout reached Mary Beth's numb brain. One of the first things the beginning riders had learned was how to get off their horses quickly if they found themselves in trouble.

Still clutching Dan's mane tightly, Mary Beth swung her right leg over the back of the saddle. At the same time, Dan abruptly halted.

Mary Beth pushed herself away from the huge horse, landing on her feet. Stumbling backward, she fell on her butt with a thump.

Andie ran up. "Hey, Finney, are you okay?"

"I'm fine, no thanks to you!" Mary Beth

snapped. Jumping up, she brushed off her jeans.

Andie bit back a grin. "Well, you weren't supposed to hit Dan *that* hard."

"You said *smack him,*" Mary Beth retorted. "And that's just what I did."

"Are you all right?" Dorothy asked as she hurried up, leading Dan.

Mary Beth nodded, her cheeks on fire. Even the dressage riders had stopped cantering, to watch her humiliation. She'd wanted to show everyone that she could control Dan. Instead, she'd gotten dumped.

"I'm fine," she told Dorothy.

Dorothy handed Andie the reins. "Walk around a few minutes to make sure," she said to Mary Beth. "Then mount up. And next time, just *tap* him lightly. Okay?"

Without looking up, Mary Beth nodded. Then she took a few steps to make sure she wasn't hurt.

Andie fell in beside her, Dan walking sedately on her left. She stuck a piece of paper under Mary Beth's nose. "This fell out of your jacket pocket when you—uh—jumped off."

Mary Beth's eyes widened. It was the letter from Brad!

13

She grabbed for it, but Andie jerked it away.

"Ooo. This must be important if Finney wants it so bad. What could it be?" Grinning mischievously, Andie unfolded the letter.

"Give that to me, you jerk," Mary Beth said, slapping at Andie's hand.

Taking two steps sideways, Andie held the letter over her head. "Come and get it!"

Furious, Mary Beth jumped into the air and snatched it from her roommate's grasp. "It's bad enough you made me fall off my horse, Andie Perez. You're not reading my letter from *Brad*."

"I did not make you fall," Andie retorted. "And why would I want to read a letter from some creep from a stupid town called Cedarville?"

Mary Beth crushed the letter in her fist. "Maybe because it's a *love* letter. To me."

Andie snorted. "Who cares?"

"You do." Mary Beth stuck her nose in Andie's face. "Because I have a boyfriend and you don't." Yanking Dan's reins away from Andie, Mary Beth stomped off toward Dorothy.

"That's telling her," Mary Beth muttered to

herself. Maybe Andie and the rest of her roommates were hotshot riders, but she, Mary Beth, had a boyfriend. Kind of. Maybe Brad wasn't exactly her boyfriend. But he was a *boy* and he was a *friend*. And he was coming for Parents' Weekend.

That was more exciting than riding a dumb old horse any day.

"So what are you going to wear for the Halloween dance on Friday?" Lauren asked Mary Beth that night. Study hours were over and all four roommates were hanging around the suite. Jina was in the shower.

Mary Beth shrugged. She was lying on her bed, dressed in baby doll pajamas with puffy sleeves. She had been trying to write a letter to Brad for the last hour.

"Who cares about the dance?" she muttered.

"We do!" Andie and Lauren chorused. Then they looked at each other and collapsed in a fit of giggles. Mary Beth thought they were nuts.

She dropped her pen and flipped over on her back. "Why? The guys from Manchester are probably geeks. Besides, who's going to dance with a bunch of sixth-graders?"

"Seventh-grade *boys,* that's who," Andie replied. Jumping off her bed, she turned up the volume on her boom box. "Watch this."

She began to move back and forth, swiveling her hips to the music. Frowning seriously, Lauren got up and tried to follow her steps. As they swayed and twisted, Andie's oversized shirt and Lauren's flannel nightie flapped like wings.

Mary Beth shook her head. "The dance of the gooney birds."

"That's for sure," Jina Williams said as she opened the bathroom door. Steam floated into the room. She wore a plaid nightshirt that highlighted her dark skin and golden eyes.

Dropping her bucket of bathroom supplies on her dresser, Jina stepped next to Lauren. "This is how it should be done."

As Jina moved gracefully to the beat, Andie and Lauren cheered and clapped. Mary Beth's mouth dropped open. She couldn't believe Jina was dancing. Usually, their roommate was so quiet.

"All right, Jina!" Andie whooped.

Jina suddenly seemed embarrassed. Blushing, she quit dancing and walked back to her dresser.

"So, how was Applejacks?" Mary Beth asked her.

Jina grinned. "Real cute, like a miniature Superstar. I watched Whitney take a lesson on him. She's a sweetie, too. She talked my ear off wanting to know all about showing."

"Hey, Jina. What costume are you going to wear to the Halloween dance Friday night?" Lauren asked.

Mary Beth rolled her eyes. Why was everyone getting so excited about a stupid dance?

Jina shrugged. "I hadn't thought much about it."

"Well, I'm not going," Mary Beth declared, flopping back over on her stomach.

"You *have* to go," Andie said. "It's required."

Mary Beth groaned. She'd forgotten about that. At Morning Meeting, Mr. Frawley, Foxhall's headmaster, had made a big deal out of all the students having to attend the weekend activities with the Manchester School.

"Well, I'm going to be a witch," Lauren said. "My mom sent me the costume already. I'm not wearing warts or a big nose, though."

Andie giggled. "Oooo. Remick's going to put a spell on some guy."

"What about *Todd?*" Mary Beth teased,

looking at Lauren over her shoulder. "Did you forget your big crush on Jina's trainer who's too old for you?"

Lauren's cheeks turned pink. "No. I just never see him now that Jina's not showing Superstar."

"A cowgirl, that's what I'll be," Jina said suddenly. She was bent over her open trunk, rooting through the stacks of clothes. Her wet hair was pulled back in a sleek ponytail. She lifted out a white shirt decorated with turquoise buttons and fringe. Holding it up, she turned to face her roommates.

"A cowgirl? That's dumb," Andie said.

"No, it's not!" Lauren jumped up and fingered the fringe. "I think it's a cool idea."

"So what are *you* going to be, Andie?" Mary Beth asked, rolling onto her side. "The bride of Frankenstein? You wouldn't need a costume for that."

"Shut up, Finney." Andie threw a smelly sock at her. "I'm going to be a Gypsy. That way I can wear lots of makeup and look mysterious. Maybe an upper-class guy will fall madly in love with me."

"He'd have to be blind and deaf," Mary

Beth joked. Holding her nose, she threw the sock back.

It hit Lauren's chest. Shrieking, she leaped away from it.

"And what are you going to be, big-mouth Finney?" Andie taunted. "With your red hair you could be Woody the Woodpecker."

"I think she'd make a perfect Anne of Green Gables," Lauren said.

"Anne of Green Gables!" Andie hooted.

Mary Beth sat up. "Hey, I love that book. But where would I get a costume?"

"That's easy. You just make it up," Jina said. She pulled a paperback off the bookshelf above her desk. It was *Anne of Green Gables*. On the cover was a red-haired girl, her chin propped in her hands. "We'll find you a straw hat and put your hair in braids."

"Oh, she'll look s-o-o-o cute," Andie teased.

"I guess," Mary Beth said doubtfully.

Lauren gave her a puzzled look. "Why don't you want to go to the dance?"

Mary Beth shook her head. "Dances are dumb, that's why." Grabbing her own bucket of bath supplies, she headed for the bathroom. "I'm brushing my teeth."

"Me, too," Lauren said. She followed Mary Beth into the bathroom where two sinks stood side by side. Next to them was a shower stall.

Mary Beth plunked her bucket down and pulled out her toothbrush and toothpaste.

"So what's wrong?" Lauren asked.

"Nothing."

"There is, too. And I want to know what it is."

Mary Beth squeezed a strip of toothpaste onto her brush and stared at Lauren in the mirror. Her friend was about a foot shorter than she was. *Cute and petite,* Mary Beth thought as she furiously scrubbed her teeth. Any boy would want to dance with Lauren.

"Remember how mad you were when I wouldn't tell you about my problem with Ashley?" Lauren persisted. Ashley Stewart, a junior and Lauren's math tutor, had ended up in the hospital because of an eating disorder. Ashley had been angry at Lauren for spilling her secret.

Mary Beth peered sideways at her friend. "This is different," she sputtered, toothpaste foaming down her chin.

"No, it's not." Lauren pouted. "I couldn't tell you about Ashley because she'd made me promise. And then she hated me because I *did* tell someone."

"At least you helped her," Mary Beth pointed out.

Lauren started to brush her teeth. When she finished, she turned to face Mary Beth. "But I *did* tell you about flunking math!" she said. "That was a big deal for me."

Mary Beth didn't know why she was so reluctant to tell Lauren what was bugging her. Her friend Janie back in Cedarville would understand. But she wasn't so sure that sweet, pretty Lauren would.

"Okay, I'll tell you," Mary Beth said finally, wiping her hands on a towel. "But promise not to tell Andie," she added.

Lauren nodded eagerly. Mary Beth pulled her over by the shower stall, away from the door.

"I don't want to go to the dance because—" she hesitated "—because I've never danced with a boy before!"

Lauren stared at Mary Beth as if she were an alien from outer space.

"I knew you wouldn't understand," Mary Beth mumbled. Pushing past Lauren, she stuck her toothbrush in her bucket.

"Wait! I do understand!" Lauren protested.

"Ha!" Mary Beth snorted. "You're so cute, tons of guys will ask you to dance. Me? I went to one party and the only guy who came up to me put ice down the back of my shirt."

"He probably knew you already had a boyfriend," Lauren said. "Why didn't you dance with Brad?"

Mary Beth flushed. What would Lauren think if she told her she'd never even been to a party with Brad?

She stared down at her bucket. "He doesn't like to dance much. Anyway, no seventh-grade guy from Manchester is going to be interested in me," she added. "I'm too tall and skinny."

"You're not any taller than Andie," Lauren pointed out.

"Yeah, but she's got a figure."

Lauren wrinkled her nose. "True. Listen, if you want to learn to dance—"

Mary Beth shook her head. "No. But thanks anyway."

"Hey! Did you two fall in the toilet?" Andie shouted as she rapped on the door. "It's almost lights-out, and I need to get in there, too."

"Remember, don't you dare tell Andie," Mary Beth whispered urgently before opening the door.

Lauren nodded solemnly. "I won't."

Twenty minutes later, Mary Beth tossed and turned in bed.

You're going to be sorry, a voice whispered in her head. *Telling all those fibs.*

Mary Beth plugged her ears. "They're not fibs," she muttered. "Brad *is* my boyfriend."

Only, Mary Beth knew he wasn't. She flopped on her side and pulled her raggedy quilt under her chin. *Tomorrow*, she decided, *I'll tell my roomates the truth. Before they find out for themselves.*

"Manchester guys? They're hunks," Stephanie, Lauren's older sister, reported at lunch the next day.

"And cool," Christina Hernandez, her roommate, added. "The guy I went out with last year had long hair and played in a band."

"A band?" Mary Beth repeated. "Which one?" She, Lauren, and Andie were listening spellbound to the older girls' stories about last year's spring dance with the Manchester School. Jina was sitting at another table, cramming for a math exam.

Stephanie and Christina exchanged amused glances, then started giggling. Mary Beth thought Lauren's sister was beautiful. She had long, silky hair and a figure like a model's. Christina was cute, too, with her dark eyes and short black hair cut in a sleek style.

"You didn't date anyone in a band, Christina," Lauren said. "You went out with that preppie-looking blond guy."

"Only because he was a senior and had a car," Christina said.

Andie scowled at the two older girls. "You two are so full of it. I don't know why we even listen to your stories."

"Because you're gullible sixth-graders," Stephanie said. "Besides, the other stuff we told you about the dance is true. All the guys wear masks and don't take them off or tell you their real names until almost the end." Standing up, she ruffled Lauren's hair before leaving. "See you later, little sis."

"Oh great. It's time for fourth period and I haven't finished lunch." Mary Beth grabbed her sandwich and started wolfing it down.

Lauren gazed dreamily across the table. "Wow, don't you think that mask stuff is romantic?"

"No!" Mary Beth said between chews. "What if the guy you're dancing with takes off his werewolf mask and he still looks like one?"

Andie laughed. "That's part of the fun."

"Sounds stupid to me," Mary Beth muttered. "I'm glad I already have a boy—"

She caught herself. *Now's the time to tell Lauren and Andie that Brad isn't your boyfriend,* she thought.

"Hey, guys." Jina came up to the table, balancing her tray on one hand. Her other hand clutched a huge stack of books.

"Ready for your math test?" Lauren asked. Mary Beth knew how glad Lauren was that she'd gotten her own exam over with last Friday.

Jina nodded. "Yup." She looked at Mary Beth, who was gulping her milk right from the carton. "Maybe tonight we can find stuff for your costume, Mary Beth," she said.

Mary Beth swallowed wrong. Lauren quickly thumped her on the back.

"Are you all right?" Jina asked.

"She's fine," Lauren answered. "She's just worried about this weekend because she can't dance. She's never even—"

"Lauren!" Mary Beth gasped, horrified.

Lauren clapped a hand over her mouth. "Whoops." She grinned sheepishly.

"That doesn't surprise me," Andie said. "We all know Finney is a klutz already."

Jina set her tray on the table. "There's nothing wrong with not being able to dance, Mary Beth. We'll practice tonight."

Mary Beth glanced back and forth at her roommates, wishing they'd leave her alone.

"Well, Finney?" Andie crossed her arms and shot her a mocking look.

Mary Beth rolled her eyes. "Okay, okay." She started to grin. "By Friday night, the girls from suite four B will knock the Manchester guys dead!"

"Heels down, back straight, relax your wrists," Mary Beth recited under her breath during her Friday afternoon lesson. As she circled Dan around Dorothy, she felt a tingle of excitement. Dan's trot was smooth and energetic. Earlier, she'd shown the whip to him, and he'd been obedient ever since.

"Heidi, your horse is falling asleep," Dorothy told the other rider. "Use that inside leg to wake him up. Shandra, every time you rise at the trot, you're hitting poor Lancelot in the mouth. Keep those hands quiet."

As Mary Beth listened to Dorothy's instructions, she smiled smugly to herself. *Ha,* she felt like telling Heidi and Shandra. For once *she* wasn't the one getting chewed out.

"Halt your horses," Dorothy said, and Dan immediately stopped dead.

"Hey. *I* didn't tell you to whoa." Mary Beth kicked him sharply with her boot heels.

Startled, Dan strode forward, his ears flicking back at Mary Beth in surprise.

"Whoa," she told him, tugging gently on the reins. This time when Dan halted, she patted his neck excitedly. He was listening to her!

When Dorothy came over, the instructor was smiling. "Very nice, Mary Beth. You're learning to be the boss."

Mary Beth grinned and held up the whip. "You were right. I didn't need to use it. Just knowing I have it made Dan listen."

"It's not just the whip making Dan respond," Dorothy reminded her. "It's you. You're feeling more confident."

Mary Beth shrugged doubtfully. "Well—"

"Walk him around the ring on a loose rein until he's a little cooler," Dorothy said as she started toward Shandra. "Then take him back to the stable and wash him off. We're ending lessons early so everyone can get ready for the big dance tonight."

Mary Beth nodded. She lengthened her reins and squeezed Dan into a walk. Head low, he ambled around the ring. Lauren and the other dressage riders had already left. Dorothy was still talking to Shandra and Heidi, so Mary Beth had one end of the ring all to herself.

Slouching in the saddle, she took a deep breath and relaxed. Her body swayed slightly as Dan walked along the rail. Today, for the first time since she'd started riding lessons, she felt in sync with Dan. It was almost like last night, when Jina had shown her some dance moves. After about half an hour, Mary Beth had been able to do them, too.

Not that it mattered, Mary Beth reminded herself. She wasn't dancing tonight anyway. If for some reason a Manchester guy *did* ask her, she'd just tell him she already had a boyfriend.

He's not really your boyfriend, Mary Beth, the nagging voice reminded her

Mary Beth narrowed her eyes, picturing Brad in her mind. He had wavy brown hair, blue eyes, and as many freckles as she had.

An idea slowly began to form in her brain. Instead of telling her roommates she'd been lying, why didn't she just ask Brad to be her boyfriend? He was already writing to her. Wasn't that proof he liked her?

Maybe when Brad came up for Parents' Weekend, she could hint around about going steady. That would solve all her problems.

"Mary Beth? Earth to Mary Beth." A voice broke into her thoughts.

"What?" Startled, Mary Beth glanced around. Lauren was perched on top of the fence rail, grinning at her. Dan had halted by the closed gate.

Mary Beth flushed. She'd been so deep in thought, she'd never even noticed that her horse had stopped!

"Are you two taking a nap?" Lauren joked.

"No. I was—uh— hoping someone would open the gate for me," Mary Beth stammered.

Lauren giggled. "Sure." She held up an envelope in her hand. "Something came in the mail for you. I wouldn't have snooped, but it looked important."

"Is it from Brad?" Mary Beth asked, her heart beginning to race.

"I don't know. There's no name on the return address, but it's from Cedarville."

Mary Beth quickly dismounted and looped the reins over Dan's head. Then she took the letter from Lauren and studied the front. "It's not my parents' writing."

"Hurry and open it!" Lauren said excitedly.

Mary Beth ripped the end off the envelope and pulled out a folded piece of paper. "Pink stationery—it can't be from Brad."

When she unfolded the letter, she looked directly at the signature. "It's from my friend Janie."

"Oh." Lauren sounded disappointed. "Well, I'm going back to the dorm," she said, climbing down from the fence. "Andie's been there all afternoon, getting ready for the dance."

"Mm," Mary Beth said, only half-listening. This was the first time Janie had written, and she was dying to find out how things were going back home.

Out of the corner of her eye, she saw Shandra and Heidi heading toward the gate, leading their horses. She'd have to read fast. Quickly, Mary Beth began to skim the letter.

Dear Mary Beth,
I have some bad news. I don't think Brad's coming to visit you Parents' Weekend. He's going steady now with Emily Zentz!

Brad and Emily! Mary Beth caught her breath.

She couldn't believe it. How could Brad have done this to her?

"What's wrong?" Lauren asked Mary Beth right after dinner. "Why aren't you getting ready for the dance?"

Mary Beth buried her face in her pillow. She didn't want to talk to Lauren. She didn't want to talk to anybody.

Lauren sat on the edge of the bed and awkwardly patted Mary Beth's shoulder. "You didn't even eat your strawberry shortcake at dinner. Did Janie write something awful in that letter?"

Mary Beth squeezed her eyes tight. She'd ripped the letter into a thousand pieces, then buried them in the manure pile behind the barn.

Lauren sighed. Mary Beth could hear Jina

and Andie talking in the bathroom. They were putting on Andie's makeup.

"You *have* to go tonight," Lauren reminded her.

"I'll tell Frawley I'm sick," Mary Beth mumbled. Punching down her pillow, she peered up at Lauren with one eye. Her friend wore a long, high-necked black witch dress. Jina had put dark mascara on Lauren's light lashes and colored her lips blood red. Mary Beth thought she looked neat in an eerie kind of way.

"I'll tell Frawley I'm about to die," Mary Beth decided.

Suddenly, Andie leaped from the bathroom, a rainbow of bright colors and glistening jewelry. "Ta-da!" she sang out, raising her arms wide. "How do I look?"

Mary Beth gazed at Andie's off-the-shoulder ruffled white blouse and red-and-yellow-striped skirt that puffed out from her waist. "Like a hot air balloon," she muttered.

Andie shot her a disgusted look. "And what are *you* dressed as?" she asked, studying Mary Beth's worn sweatpants and sweatshirt. "A pile of dirty clothes?"

"I think you're a great Gypsy, Andie," Lauren said. Andie's hair swirled wildly around her bare shoulders. She wore several gold chains around her neck, blue eyeshadow, and big hoop earrings. "And you look super, too, Jina," Lauren added.

"Thanks." Jina had on her fringed shirt, jeans, and the navy-blue cowboy boots her mother had sent in the mail.

"I can't wait! This dance is major excitement at boring old Foxhall." Andie twirled in a circle. Flopping down on the bed, she snatched up Mary Beth's hand. "Let me tell your fortune," she said. "You will meet a mysterious young man."

Mary Beth yanked her hand out of Andie's grasp. "I already know my fortune," she retorted, tears springing into her eyes. "And there's no young man in my future."

Lauren's mouth dropped open. "So that's what's bugging you. Janie must have written that Brad dumped you!"

Mary Beth jerked her chin around. "*Thanks* for telling everyone, Lauren."

"I just guessed," Lauren replied huffily. "You don't have to bite my head off."

"So what if Brad the geek dumped you?" Andie chimed in as she gazed at her reflection

34

in the mirror. "Now you'll have to come to the dance, so you can meet some cool guy."

"Andie's right," Jina agreed. "It's better than moping around the suite."

Mary Beth sniffed loudly. "Oh, all right," she said. Actually, things hadn't worked out that badly, she decided suddenly. Since Brad wasn't coming for Parents' weekend, she wouldn't have to tell her roommates that he was never her boyfriend in the first place.

Sitting up, she reached for the straw hat that she'd borrowed from a girl down the hall and for the white apron that one of the cafeteria ladies had loaned her. She held the apron against her chest and plopped the hat on her head. "How do I look?"

"Weird," Andie replied. "I don't think you'll have to worry about anyone asking you to dance."

"Good," Mary Beth said. "I don't ever want to speak to another boy for as long as I live!"

"I can't believe it," Mary Beth muttered as she stared at her image in the mirror. She and Jina were standing in the girls' room down the hall from the gym. "It looks as though someone squashed a giant strawberry on my cheeks."

Jina laughed. "Lauren did go a little crazy with the face paint. But I like your braids."

"You're kidding." Mary Beth wrinkled her nose in disgust. *Weird* was definitely the right word to describe the way she looked.

Just then the door opened and sounds of music and laughter floated into the bathroom. Two seventh grade girls came in, their arms linked, their heads bent as they giggled together. One was dressed like Dorothy from *The Wizard of Oz*. The other was dressed like Toto.

When the girls disappeared into the stalls, Mary Beth whispered to Jina, "Do you think we're the only ones having a horrible time?"

"Nah." Jina adjusted her cowgirl hat, which kept slipping sideways. "There must be others."

"Well, at least the food is good," Mary Beth said with a sigh. "Why don't we stuff some goodies in my apron pockets to take back to the suite? We have to hang around fifteen more minutes before we can leave."

"Good idea." Jina followed Mary Beth out into the dimly lit hall. Costumed couples huddled in the darkened corners, whispering together.

At the doorway to the gym, Mary Beth paused. The ceiling of the huge room was hung with black and orange streamers and white yarn woven like cobwebs. Jack-o'-lanterns grinned from the tops of bales of hay, and stuffed-pillowcase ghosts floated in the corners.

"Do you see Lauren or Andie anywhere?" Jina asked. She was standing on tiptoe, searching across the crowded gym.

Mary Beth studied the mass of gyrating bodies. Masked dancers moved to the beat of a local rock band that played on the stage. It was impossible to tell who was who.

"No. Wait, there's Lauren, I think." Mary Beth pointed to the left. A petite girl dressed in black was dancing with a boy in a vampire costume. Her pointed hat wobbled and dipped as she spun in a circle. "That's got to be her. I don't think there were many other witches tonight."

"She's been with that same vampire all night," Jina said.

"Not like Andie. Every time I see her she's dancing with a different guy."

Mary Beth and Jina headed toward the refreshment table. A half-dozen teachers stood around talking and sipping punch. In the corner, several boys were hanging out together. They were laughing and punching one another, looking very uncomfortable.

Manchester guys aren't so cool, Mary Beth thought. As she munched on a potato chip, she studied them out of the corner of her eye. One of the boys had a great costume. He was dressed all in black with shiny, high boots, tight pants, and a long-sleeved shirt with a flowing cape. A brimmed hat was pulled low over his forehead, and a mask covered his eyes.

Just as Mary Beth was stuffing another chip into her mouth, the boy in black turned and stared at her. Startled, she sucked in her breath, and a piece of chip caught in her windpipe. Coughing furiously, she doubled over.

"Are you all right?" Jina asked worriedly. She pounded Mary Beth on the back.

Just totally embarrassed, Mary Beth thought as she gagged and coughed for the second time that day. She hoped the guy in black wasn't noticing.

"A chip went down the wrong way," Mary Beth gasped finally. "I'm okay."

Jina nodded and began to spoon peanuts

into a napkin. "Ready to go?" she asked.

"Sure. But don't you want to dance before we leave? You're such a good dancer."

Jina shrugged. "Not really. I've got better things to do than think about boys. Maybe when I'm older."

"Oh." Mary Beth grabbed a handful of M&M's and dropped them in her pocket. She wished she could think the same way as Jina.

She blinked back tears as she suddenly remembered about Brad and Emily Zentz. She'd been a total dummy to think Brad would ever want to go steady with her.

Hastily, Mary Beth wiped her cheeks with the sleeve of her blouse, leaving a smear of red makeup on the flowered print.

"Let's hurry up and get out of here," she said to Jina. "What else do you want to take back to the suite?"

"Definitely onion dip," Jina said, pointing to the bowl on the table.

Mary Beth grimaced. "That'll make a real mess in my pocket."

"Put it in a punch cup," Jina suggested. "I'll get crackers and two pieces of cake for dessert."

"Okay." Mary Beth reached for an orange-striped cup. Using a cracker, she scooped out some dip, licking several blobs off her fingers. It was delicious.

"Hey, don't hog all the dip," someone said.

Mary Beth swung around. The boy in the cool black costume was standing right behind her.

Was he talking to her?

"Uh, right," Mary Beth stammered nervously, her fingers tightening around the paper cup. Suddenly gooey dip splurted from the top like lava from a volcano. Mary Beth watched in horror as dip slid down the side of the cup and plopped on top of the boy's shiny boots.

Slowly, she looked up at him. His mouth hung open in disbelief and his fake mustache quivered.

Mary Beth's cheeks grew hot.

"Hi," she croaked stupidly. "I'm Mary Beth. Would you like to dance?"

5

The boy's dark brows shot up under the brim of his hat. "Dance? I don't think I can. *Someone* just spilled dip on my boot."

Mary Beth's face felt even warmer. "Oh, right. Sorry." Turning, she grabbed some napkins off the table. Her gaze shot wildly around the room. *Where was Jina?*

"I'll clean it up," Mary Beth told the boy quickly. Too embarrassed to look at him, Mary Beth bent over and swiped at the creamy dip, smearing it across the top of his boot.

"Gee, thanks," the boy said. "Look, I'll do it, okay?" He took a napkin from Mary Beth and stepped away from her. Then, lifting up his boot, he finished wiping off the dip. Mary Beth mopped up the floor, then stood up, clutching the gooey napkin.

"Ready to go?" Jina came up beside her, holding a plate of cake.

"Yes!" Mary Beth blurted. She'd never been so happy to see someone in her life.

"Hey," the boy in black said. "I thought you asked me to dance."

"I did?" Mary Beth squeaked.

"You did?" Jina stared at her in surprise.

The boy nodded. "She did. Right after she spilled dip on my foot."

Jina looked back and forth between the two of them, her expression puzzled.

Mary Beth smiled dumbly. "I did."

The boy in black folded his arms across his chest. "Well? Are we going to dance?"

Mary Beth's smile faded. She couldn't believe this was happening. Her gaze darted toward Jina. "Is it okay with you?"

Jina grinned reassuringly. "Sure. If I'm not here when you're done, it means I've probably gone back to the dorm with some of the other girls."

Mary Beth glanced sideways at the boy in black. He was as tall as she was, with brown hair.

A thrill of excitement tingled up Mary

Beth's arms. *He's kind of cute,* she thought. *Cuter than Brad—I think.* It was hard to tell.

A fast song started. Mary Beth reached out and squeezed Jina's wrist. "I'll see you later," she whispered, as the boy in black took her hand and pulled her onto the dance floor.

I'm really going to dance with a guy! Mary Beth thought excitedly as she followed him into the crowd. But when he stopped in front of a bunch of kids and started dancing, Mary Beth froze. Her body felt like a wooden board. She'd forgotten everything that Jina had taught her.

Move your arms, stupid, she told herself.

Mary Beth looked around. Everybody was doing something different.

Mary Beth swung her arms to the left, suddenly noticing she was still clutching the sticky napkin. She shoved it in her apron pocket. Then, wiping her fingers on her skirt, she tried to copy the other dancers' moves. The band swung into a song she recognized, and her body began moving on its own to the beat.

Finally, she peeked at her partner. He grinned at her. Relieved, she grinned back. This was fun!

When the band took a break and the music stopped, he leaned toward her. "So who are you supposed to be?" he asked.

"Guess."

He shot her a pained look. "I don't know. Raggedy Ann with measles? My sister has a doll that looks like you."

Mary Beth plopped her hands on her hips. "Haven't you ever heard of Anne of Green Gables?"

"Is it a video game?" he teased.

She rolled her eyes.

"All right, if you're so smart, guess who I am." He looped his thumb in his belt, striking a dramatic pose.

"Hmm." Mary Beth studied him for a moment. "Batman doesn't wear a hat. And the Lone Ranger doesn't wear a cape."

"I'm Zorro," he said impatiently.

"Who's Zorro?"

"You don't know who Zorro is?" he repeated incredulously. "He was the defender of the poor. Didn't you ever see the Walt Disney show?"

"That was Robin Hood," Mary Beth protested. "And he wore green—not black!"

"Mary Beth!" a shout interrupted. Andie

was crossing the gym floor toward them. Mary Beth suddenly realized that she and Zorro were standing by themselves. Most of the other dancers had wandered over to the food tables or out into the hall.

Andie's eyes widened when she saw Mary Beth's partner. "Uh, hi, Mary Beth," she said, her gaze not leaving Zorro's. Her dark eyes sparkled mischievously, her hair stuck out in a wild veil, and one of her earrings was missing. "Having fun?"

"Yes," Mary Beth said. *Now go away,* she added to herself. The last thing she needed to hear was one of Andie's snide comments.

Andie turned to Mary Beth and winked. "Cute," she mouthed. Then, after waving at someone by the gym door, she ran off.

"Would you like something to eat?" Zorro asked.

Mary Beth looked over at the food tables. They were surrounded by kids. "Sure, but it's pretty crowded over there." She reached into her pocket. "How about some M&M's? Oops." That one held a sticky napkin. She checked the other pocket. "Here."

She passed him a handful of candy, and they munched in silence. Mary Beth tried to think of something clever to say. She was dying to ask him his name, but she remembered the boys weren't supposed to reveal their identities until the end of the dance.

"So, what grade are you in?" she asked finally.

He swallowed a mouthful of candy.

"Seventh. How about you?" he asked.

"Sixth." Mary Beth reached for the last of the M&M's. "So are those riding boots I dropped dip on?"

"Yeah. I'm in Manchester's riding program."

"Me, too!" Mary Beth exclaimed. "I mean, I'm in Foxhall's riding program."

"Are you competing in the games tomorrow?"

She nodded. "It's required."

"Same here. But it should be fun. Manchester's pretty psyched up to beat Foxhall in the school race. The girls-against-the-guys rivalry has been going on for years. Foxhall won last year."

"Well, I won't be in that race," Mary Beth admitted. "Only the—" *Only the best riders are in it,* she was about to say. Instead, she shoved a handful of M&M's in her mouth. No need to tell Zorro that she was just a beginning rider.

The lights dimmed again and the band started tuning up. Zorro reached for her hand. "Want to dance some more?"

Mary Beth nodded eagerly. She wiped her palm on her apron, streaking red M&M coloring down the front, then slipped her fingers in his.

Once again the dance floor grew crowded. Mary Beth and Zorro danced for another half hour. Then the band quit and a spotlight hit the stage.

A man dressed in a gorilla costume came onstage. He took off his gorilla head, and the crowd of students hooted and clapped when they saw it was Mr. Frawley, Foxhall's headmaster. He tapped on the microphone, then cleared his throat.

"Ladies and gentlemen, ghouls and goblins," he began. "It is now the witching hour, when our visitors from the Manchester School must unmask and reveal their true identities."

Mary Beth glanced nervously at Zorro, who stood on her left. In the dim light, she could barely see his profile. She wondered what he would look like without his mask, fake mustache, and hat.

The band began a drumroll. Zorro looked

over at her, and Mary Beth flushed.

"Kill the lights!" Mr. Frawley said, and the room went even darker.

Mary Beth held her breath. Bodies jostled her from all sides. "Zorro?" she whispered. "Are you there?"

Just then, the lights flashed on. Mary Beth blinked rapidly. In the spot where Zorro had been standing, a girl in a pink poodle skirt and beehive hairdo was embracing a guy dressed as Big Bird.

Mary Beth spun to her right. A guy in a motorcycle jacket was kissing a butterfly.

"Zorro?" Mary Beth called. Someone bumped into her, and she stumbled sideways. The band started playing again. Two ghosts, their arms linked, floated past as the crowd began to sing.

Mary Beth pushed her way around the butterfly, searching the bobbing dancers for the boy dressed in black.

But Zorro was nowhere in sight.

6

Mary Beth couldn't believe it. Where had Zorro gone?

"Mary Beth!" Someone reached around a dancing giraffe and grabbed her hand. Mary Beth glimpsed a black sleeve. She breathed a sigh of relief.

She'd found him!

"Excuse me," Mary Beth shouted, ducking under the giraffe's neck. A witch pulled her close and hugged her excitedly.

"You decided to stay!" Lauren yelled into Mary Beth's ear. "Are you having fun?"

"I was." Mary Beth pulled back to look at her roommate. Lauren was still dancing with the vampire. He'd taken out his fangs and pulled off his mask, revealing a blond boy about their age with blue eyes and dimples.

Lauren pulled Mary Beth closer. "Where s the guy in black you were dancing with?"

"He disappeared."

Lauren's eyes widened. "Wow. He really was mysterious. Did you find out his name?"

Mary Beth shook her head. "Maybe I'll see him at the games tomorrow."

If I recognize him, she added to herself. *Or he recognizes me.* Waving goodbye to Lauren, Mary Beth pushed through the costumed dancers until she reached the door. Before she left, she gazed across the gym one last time.

Just in case he hasn't left, she told herself. Maybe he'd gotten lost in the crowd and was hunting for her.

Mary Beth doubted it. When the lights had gone off, he'd ducked out on purpose.

Dejectedly, she turned and walked into the hall. Zorro had decided he didn't want her to know who he really was. That way, he wouldn't have to see her again this weekend.

Sighing, she shoved her hand in her apron pocket—right into something warm and mushy.

Yuck. She jerked her hand out. The wadded-up napkin was stuck to her fingers.

Disgusted, she threw it into a nearby trash

can and stomped down the hallway to the exit door.

What a dumb dance, she decided, yanking out the rubber bands that held her braids. She should have gone back to the suite with Jina. Then she never would have met Zorro.

Not that she cared if she ever saw him again. Or Brad.

Or any other guy in the whole world. Ever.

"Do you see him? Do you see Zorro?" Lauren asked as she and Mary Beth led their horses around the busy courtyard. The stable area was filled with students getting their horses ready for the games.

It was a chilly, overcast Saturday morning. The Manchester students had arrived by bus for a joint brunch in the Foxhall dining room. Afterward, all the riders met at the stables.

Since the Manchester students and faculty had been assigned Foxhall horses, Mary Beth was sharing Dan with Dr. Kresky, Manchester's headmaster. Luckily, he only needed to ride Dan into the ring at the beginning of the games to announce the different teams.

"No, I don't see him," Mary Beth said. Halting Dan, she glared at Lauren, who was holding Whisper's reins. "And I'm *not* looking for him, either."

"Why not?" Lauren peered around Whisper's head. She was dressed in her new, tight-fitting leggings, high black boots, a striped turtleneck sweater, and a blue windbreaker.

Mary Beth had thrown on old jeans and her corduroy jacket and pulled her hair into a ponytail. She didn't care how she looked.

"Because," Mary Beth told her roommate for the tenth time, "I don't want to see him again. Besides, I've got something else to worry about—riding in these stupid games. What is the egg race, anyway?"

"You put an egg on a spoon, then ride around the ring," Lauren explained. "The person whose egg stays on the spoon the longest wins."

Mary Beth groaned. "That sounds mega-dumb. Is there a booby prize for the person who drops their egg first?"

Just then, Andie came up riding Ranger, the Foxhall horse she'd been assigned until she could ride Magic. He was a tall, sixteen-three hand bay gelding with lots of energy.

"Hey, guys." Andie wore chaps over her jeans, paddock boots, and a heavy red sweater.

Ranger halted right in front of Mary Beth. Sticking his nose out, he rubbed it on her shoulder, knocking her into Dan's neck.

"Go away, Ranger," Mary Beth said, pushing his big head. He snorted, blowing snot everywhere.

"Gross!" Mary Beth wiped her cheek on her sleeve.

Andie chuckled. "You're such a wimp, Finney. Hey, did you guys hear the good news? I get to ride in the school race!"

"Wow!" Lauren exclaimed. "How'd you manage that? I thought they weren't letting sixth-graders race."

Andie shrugged. "They knew I was the best." She leaned over Ranger's neck toward Lauren. "So, did you see old Chaddie this morning?"

Lauren flushed. "At the brunch. But Chad's not a rider. He's playing in the coed soccer game."

"What about you, Andie?" Mary Beth said. "Did you see Sam? Or was it Harry—no, Roger? Or wait, I remember now—you ended up with Paul last night."

"They were all crazy about me," Andie bragged. "And you should see the guy I'm

53

sharing Ranger with, Jeff." She whistled. "An eighth-grader and he's gorgeous."

Mary Beth rolled her eyes. "Go jump in manure, Andie. Where's Jina?"

"She's over with some dorky sixth-grader named Tommy," Andie said. "She's sharing Three Bars Jake with him for the games."

"Foxhall and Manchester students!" someone announced loudly.

Mary Beth turned. Mrs. Caufield, the head riding instructor, was striding across the courtyard, yelling through a bullhorn. "It's time to begin the games. Everyone needs to meet at the lower outdoor ring."

"I'm out of here." Andie steered Ranger to the left. As she rode him through the crowd, he danced sideways, his black tail swishing.

"Oh, great." Mary Beth exhaled loudly. "Here goes disaster. Come on, Dan." Clucking, she led the big horse down the drive.

"Lighten up, Mary Beth," Lauren said cheerfully as she and Whisper fell into step beside them. "The games will be fun. Dan's so steady, you'll do great. Do you have your riding whip?"

Mary Beth held it up, showing the aid to Dan. Immediately, his ears pricked alertly.

"Don't get lazy on me," she warned him.

When they reached the ring, she scanned the milling groups of kids and horses. "I'm supposed to find Dr. Kresky and help him mount Dan," she told Lauren.

Her roommate started to giggle. "Just hope you don't have to give him a leg up."

When Mary Beth finally spied Dr. Kresky, she realized what Lauren meant. The Manchester headmaster was bursting out of his tight breeches. His stomach bulged under his black riding coat.

"I didn't think breeches stretched that far," Mary Beth said, giggling. "Well, I'll see you later. Maybe we'll be on the same team."

When Mary Beth and Dan reached Dr. Kresky, the headmaster was nervously tapping a riding crop against his boot.

"Ah, my steed!" he said when he saw Dan.

"Thank you, Mary Beth." Mrs. Caufield bustled up and took Dan's reins. "I'll help Dr. Kresky."

Not sure what to do, Mary Beth headed over to the jump standard where the games lists were posted. She'd signed up for the egg race, and she'd also ride later in the relay race.

In a few minutes, Dr. Kresky would

announce the teams. They'd been chosen by the head riding instructors of the two schools. Each team was a mix of beginning and advanced riders. Points would be given to riders in each event—from first place, which earned six points, all the way down to sixth place, which earned one point. Each rider's points would be assigned to his or her team. The team with the highest total would win.

Mary Beth stopped in front of the list, just as Jina walked up leading Three Bars Jake, a chunky quarter horse. She wore a suede jacket over her tan sweater and schooling breeches.

A dark-haired boy wearing chaps, jeans, and a baggy bomber jacket walked beside Jake. Mary Beth figured he must be Tommy.

"What event are you riding in?" Jina asked.

"The egg race." Mary Beth pointed to her name on the list. "Andie's in bareback dollar and the school race. What about you?"

"The obstacle race," Jina replied. "And the pairs race with Lauren."

"I'm in the obstacle race, too," the boy said. Mary Beth glanced at him. He definitely looked like a sixth-grader.

"Hi, I'm Tommy," he said, smiling shyly.

"Hi," Mary Beth said, smiling back. "I'm

Mary Beth Finney."

Just then, Andie rode up on Ranger. "Hey, Jina, did you hear I'm in the school race?" She patted Ranger soundly on the neck. "Old Caufield wanted to make sure Foxhall would beat Manchester." When she said the other school's name, she gave Tommy a triumphant look.

He laughed. "Foxhall may have won last year, but I bet Manchester will take the race this year."

Andie snorted. "I doubt it."

"Attention, students!" Dr. Kresky blasted through the bullhorn. He was mounted on Dan, who stood patiently in the middle of the ring. The headmaster's rear was so wide it enveloped the small saddle.

"Wow." Andie giggled. "I never thought I'd see a butt bigger than Dan's."

Mary Beth laughed as she moved to the rail around the ring so she could hear better. Jina stood on her left side, Tommy on her right.

"We will now announce the teams for the day's events." Dr. Kresky held up a piece of paper.

"On the red team are Andie Perez, Alicia Sachs, Michael Whelan, Mary Beth Finney, and captain Tommy Isaacson."

"Uh-oh," Tommy muttered.

Mary Beth looked over at him. He gulped nervously, his Adam's apple bobbing in his neck.

Andie brought Ranger up beside him. "*You're* Tommy Isaacson?" she asked, looking down from her horse.

He nodded.

"And *you're* the captain?" she asked, her voice dripping with disbelief.

He nodded again, staring at his riding boots.

Andie hit her forehead with the palm of her hand. "Great. A wimpy sixth-grader as a captain."

"Shut up, Andie," Mary Beth said. "We're sixth-graders too, remember?" She couldn't believe her roommate was being such a jerk.

"I was only joking, Finney," Andie retorted. "If I really wanted to be uncool, I'd complain about being on the team with *you*!"

"Me?" Mary Beth said angrily. Tommy had quit looking at his feet and was staring at her. Even Jina had turned around.

"That's right," Andie said. "With you on our team, we're bound to lose!"

Mary Beth fought back tears. "That was really mean, Andie," she retorted. Jina's mouth had dropped open. Tommy was staring at her as if she were a freak.

Andie's eyes widened. "Hey, can't you take a joke, Finney?" she asked. "Sure you're a lousy rider, but I still like you."

Mary Beth stepped next to Ranger's side, and glared up at Andie. "You just watch. I'll win *lots* of points for our team. More than you!"

"Hey, don't take it so hard," Andie said. "I mean, I'm sorry." She squeezed her leg against Ranger's side. He stepped sideways, swinging his powerful hindquarters toward Mary Beth. She jumped backward just in time.

"Whoa." Andie pulled on the reins.

Dr. Kresky was still announcing the other teams, but Mary Beth didn't want to listen. Too embarrassed to even look at Jina and Tommy, she shoved her way past two Manchester students and escaped into the crowd.

What a jerk Andie is, she thought. Usually, she could take her roommate's teasing. But not today. Not after Janie's letter about Brad and Zorro's ditching her at the dance.

Fists clenched, she almost marched into Whisper, with Lauren in the saddle,

"Where are you going in such a hurry?" Lauren asked.

"To get my horse before that fat Kresky squashes him flat," Mary Beth said angrily. She shaded her eyes, and looked up at her friend. Dressed in her new riding outfit, Lauren looked totally cute. Her heels were down, legs in the right position, and her back was straight, yet relaxed.

Mary Beth scowled at her.

"What's wrong with you *now*?" Lauren asked, obviously puzzled. "Did you find Zorro and he pretended he didn't know who you are? Is that what's bugging you?"

"No!" Mary Beth replied forcefully. "And I told you before, I'm not looking for him. Andie just called me a lousy rider in front of Jina and some guy. Well, I'm going to prove I'm not by winning that stupid egg race—even if I have to hardboil my egg!"

"The trick to keeping the egg from falling out of the spoon is to keep your horse slow and steady—no matter what the gait," Tommy told Mary Beth, as the two of them stood by the ring's in gate, half an hour later. They each wore red arm bands around the sleeves of their jackets. The egg race was the first event.

"You know, you don't have to take this captain stuff so seriously," Mary Beth said. Dan dozed beside her. Mary Beth wished she could relax, too.

Why had she shot off her big mouth again to Lauren? There was no way she'd win this event.

Tommy shrugged. "Being captain's no big deal. But your roommate made me mad, too." He scuffed his toe in the dust. "You know, that crack about being a wimpy sixth-grader."

Mary Beth grinned at him. "Andie makes everybody mad. One night she even dropped her dinner tray on Mr. Frawley, our headmaster, on purpose. He went nuts."

Tommy laughed, and for a moment, Mary Beth forgot about the race.

"If she went to our school, she would have been kicked out for that," Tommy said. "Manchester is pretty strict." Leaning forward, he rested his elbows on the top of the gate. Mary Beth thought he was nice, for a guy.

He wasn't dashing and handsome like Zorro, she decided. Or funny like Brad. But nice was okay.

She tucked a stray strand of hair back under her riding helmet. "So you have a million rules at Manchester, too?"

"A million and one," Tommy said grimly. "And tons of homework. Sometimes I wish I was going to school back home. My friends don't have half the work."

Mary Beth nodded. "I know what you mean. My friend Janie writes about roller-skating and watching TV and hanging around at the mall during the school week. I write her back about study hour and lights-out."

"All riders for the egg race, please enter the ring," Mrs. Caufield announced with the bullhorn.

Mary Beth jumped. "Oops, that's me," she said nervously.

"Oh, Captain Tom," Andie called sweetly as she came up with Michael and Alicia, the other members of the red team. Michael, a freshman at Manchester, was wearing expensive cowboy boots and a hat. Alicia, a junior from Foxhall, competed in dressage with Lauren.

"Did you instruct Mary Beth on a winning strategy?" Andie asked Tommy.

Tommy grinned. "You bet. She's going to run into all the other riders and knock their eggs off their spoons."

Andie nodded seriously. "Good plan. Jeff, the guy I'm sharing Ranger with, is riding in the egg race, too." She snickered. "I told him that Ranger's lazy and to give him a good kick when they have to trot."

"Andie!" Mary Beth exclaimed. "Ranger will take off if Jeff kicks him hard."

"That's the idea!" Andie said gleefully.

Mrs. Caufield opened the gate. Mary Beth gathered her reins and Andie gave her a leg up on Dan. She handed her whip to Andie.

"I won't be able to hold this."

Andie waved the whip in front of Dan's face. His big head jerked up. "Dan, you do what Mary Beth says," she warned him, "or *I'll* ride you in the next event."

"That threat should shape him up," Tommy said to Mary Beth in a low voice.

She laughed. Then, taking a deep breath, she squeezed Dan's sides with her legs, urging him toward the ring along with a dozen other horses and riders. All of the riders were wearing different colored arm bands. As each one of them went in, Mrs. Caufield handed him or her a spoon and egg.

Mary Beth was glad she'd learned how to hold the reins in her left hand while holding a whip in the right. She took the spoon and egg in her right hand, and then steered Dan toward the railing. When she passed Michael, Andie, Alicia, and Tommy, they all gave her the thumbs-up sign.

"Go, red team!" Andie cheered.

"All right, riders," Mrs. Caufield called, "place your egg in your spoon. When the bell rings, the race will begin. If your egg falls, come into the center of the ring."

"Okay, Dan. Here goes nothing," Mary Beth muttered. She dropped the reins briefly and gingerly set the egg on her spoon. Then, keeping her gaze directed on the egg, she picked the reins back up with her left hand.

Dan yawned and walked steadily along the rail. The bell rang and Mary Beth's heart flip-flopped.

This was it!

"All walk," Mrs. Caufield called.

A girl riding a high-spirited gray named Lukas jigged past. Her horse sashayed in front of Dan. He didn't even blink. The girl's egg fell with a plop. "Oops," she said. Laughing, she turned the gray into the middle of the ring.

"Go, Mary Beth!" Lauren and Jina yelled from ringside. Mary Beth smiled slightly, but kept her eyes directed on her spoon. Lauren and Jina were both on the blue team. She wasn't going to let them distract her.

"All riders halt."

"Whoa, Dan," Mary Beth said in her deepest voice. He stopped dead. Her egg wobbled, then settled in the spoon. Two more riders went into the middle of the ring.

"Trot. All riders trot."

Mary Beth's heart leaped into her throat. *Slow and steady*, Tommy had warned. That was Dan's specialty—if she could get him to go.

"Remember what Andie said, Dan," she reminded him. "Trot!" she commanded sternly, squeezing him hard with her calves. He walked two strides, then broke into a smooth, easy jog. Slowly, Mary Beth posted, her gaze riveted on her egg.

"Up, down. Up, down," she recited, pretending this was a lesson.

Beside her, she heard a loud snort, and Ranger charged past. Jeff was holding onto the mane with one hand, the reins with the other. His spoon and egg were nowhere in sight.

"Up, down. Up, down." Mary Beth forced herself not to look at Jeff.

The egg jiggled. Mary Beth held her breath.

"You're doing great, Finney!" someone hollered.

Teeth clenched, fingers tight on her spoon, Mary Beth concentrated on one thing—*the egg*.

"Reverse at a trot," Mrs. Caufield called.

Mary Beth dug her left heel into Dan's side, signaling him to cross the ring so they could reverse direction. Loud cheering broke out along the rail. Dan jogged past Mrs. Caufield and the growing line of riders now in the middle of the ring.

"Mary Beth Finney—into the center of the ring!" Mrs. Caufield blasted through her bullhorn.

Mary Beth frowned. But her egg hadn't fallen!

Confused, she looked up. Mrs. Caufield was waving a blue ribbon in the air. Mary Beth glanced around, suddenly realizing she was the only one still trotting.

Mrs. Caufield turned the bullhorn toward the crowd outside the ring. "First place and six points go to Mary Beth Finney on the red team!"

Dan stopped dead in his tracks and Mary Beth hit the pommel with a thump. Her egg flew into the air, landing on the ground with a crack.

Mary Beth couldn't believe it.

She'd won!

"Way to go, Finney! All right, red team!" Andie cheered hysterically.

Mary Beth grinned from ear to ear as she turned Dan toward Mrs. Caufield. The riding director pinned the blue ribbon on the side of the big horse's brow band. He tossed his head, making the ribbon flap.

Okay, so it's not like I won at some big deal horse show, Mary Beth told herself. But still it was first place in something!

"Nice job, Mary Beth," Mrs. Caufield congratulated her. Then, raising the bullhorn, she announced the second-place winner.

Mary Beth was too excited to listen. "We did it, you clod." Bending over Dan's neck, she gave him a hug as he ambled toward the exit gate.

Andie ran up and grabbed Dan's reins. "What skill, what daring, what nerves of steel," she joked.

"What baloney," Mary Beth shot right back. "But, hey, I did it, didn't I? Six big points for our team." She slid off Dan, then looked around. "Where's Tommy?"

"Captain Wimpy's getting ready for the obstacle race. I still can't believe they made him captain. I bet he can't even ride."

That remark made Mary Beth fume. Tommy was a nice guy. "I'll take that bet," she countered.

"You're on." Andie tossed her hair behind her shoulders. "If he doesn't get a first or second in the obstacle race, *you* can do my math homework for a week!"

"And what do I get if I win?"

Andie leaned closer. "*Maybe* you'll finally get a boyfriend. Captain Wimpy seems to like you." With another toss of her hair, she walked off.

"I don't want a boyfriend!" Mary Beth hollered after her.

Andie ignored her. Mary Beth rolled her eyes. *Why do you always make stupid bets with Andie?* she scolded herself. *She always wins.*

Turning, Mary Beth led Dan away from the crowded ring. She stopped him on a grassy strip and loosened his girth. Immediately, he put his head down to eat.

"Stop it, Dan!" she scolded, jerking on the reins.

"Great job, Mary Beth!" Lauren ran up, beaming. A blue band circled her arm.

Mary Beth looked suspiciously at her. "Why are you so glad the red team won?"

Lauren laughed. "You're as bad as Andie. Can you believe she told Jeff to *kick* Ranger? Luckily, he's on the yellow team. The blue team came in second in the egg race," she rushed on excitedly. "And now Jina's riding in the obstacle race. She should get first place easily."

"Oh, great." Mary Beth blew a strand of hair off her cheek. She secured the stirrup irons, then turned to face Lauren. "I made a bet with Andie that our team captain, Tommy, would win. I forgot Jina was in the obstacle race."

"So are Ginny and Missy," Lauren said, naming two other Foxhall riders. "They're both super riders."

Mary Beth groaned. "Looks like I'll be

doing Andie's homework for a week."

"All riders for the obstacle race come into the ring!" Mrs. Caufield called through the bullhorn.

"Let's watch!" Lauren tugged on Mary Beth's jacket sleeve. "This should be fun!"

"Right," Mary Beth said, without enthusiasm. Leading Dan, she followed Lauren past the other horses and riders until they reached the ring. The two of them leaned on the top rail, while Dan promptly cocked his back leg and fell asleep.

Mary Beth immediately spotted Jina, who was mounted on Jake. Tommy was riding the gray that had almost dumped the girl in the egg race.

"Oh, no!" Mary Beth said. "Tommy's riding Lukas. He'll never win now."

"He was supposed to share Jake with Jina, but since they're in the same event, Caufield assigned him Lukas." Lauren shook her head. "Tough break."

Lukas was a beautiful but flighty Anglo-Arabian. Mary Beth knew Alicia often had trouble with him during her dressage lessons.

"There's David Parkerson on Whisper," Lauren said. She pointed to a tall boy who

71

looked as though he could be a basketball player. His legs hung way down Whisper's sides, and a yellow band circled his arm. "He's a senior at Manchester. My sister dated him a couple of times last year. I don't think he's much of a rider."

Mary Beth scanned the ring while the riders listened to Mrs. Caufield explain the rules. A small jump, a mailbox, a piece of plywood, and a tarp had been set on the ground at different points in the ring. Right in front of dozing Dan were two poles placed parallel to each other, about three feet apart.

Lauren pointed to the tarp. "David will *never* get Whisper to walk over that."

"They have to walk over it?" Mary Beth asked.

"They just have to get over it somehow. They also have to put a letter in the mailbox, trot over the jump, get across the plywood, then back their horse between the two poles and out the other side. The pair who can do all of that with the fastest time wins."

Mary Beth whistled. "It's good thing Dan and I didn't enter." She glanced over her shoulder. "I wonder where Andie is."

Lauren giggled. "Probably putting burrs

under the other teams' saddle pads. There go Whisper and David!" she added, punching Mary Beth on the arm to make her look.

Neck-reining Whisper, David steered the chestnut mare toward the first obstacle, the mailbox. He jerked on the bit to make her stop, then reached to open the mailbox door.

Immediately, Whisper stuck her nose in the air and danced sideways. David pulled her roughly around, and digging his heel into her side, tried to move her back to the mailbox.

Lauren grimaced. "Oh, boy. He's doing everything Whisper hates," she told Mary Beth.

"This is going to be a disaster."

"Good. Then the yellow team won't win."

Mary Beth watched as Whisper planted her hooves and refused to move any closer to the mailbox. Finally, David gave up and trotted her toward the tarp.

Neck arched, Whisper eyed the tarp suspiciously. David gave her a kick. The mare pranced about four feet from the tarp's edge, gathered her legs under her, and leaped. The crowd laughed, then applauded as David grabbed Whisper's mane to keep from falling off.

Next, the pair trotted to the crossbar. This time, David stayed with the mare as she sailed over the bar, clearing it by a mile.

"Wow. I didn't know Whisper could jump," Mary Beth said.

"Yeah," Lauren said flatly.

"So why don't you ever jump her?" Mary Beth asked.

Her roommate shrugged. "I don't know. Oh look, here comes the plywood."

By this time, David was grinning good-naturedly as Foxhall and Manchester students cheered him on. Horse and rider approached the plywood, Whisper flicking her ears nervously. David held tight to the mane with both hands. Whisper jumped onto the plywood, her hooves making a thudding noise. Frightened by the sound, she leaped off sideways.

Lauren shook her head. "I don't think that performance is going to win first place."

"Jina's next," Mary Beth said. "She and Jake should do great."

Jina trotted the spunky quarter horse to the mailbox. He stopped right in front of it and waited patiently while she opened the door and stuck in the letter. Just as smoothly, he trotted to the tarp, walked over it, jumped the small fence, and calmly walked over the board.

Mary Beth groaned. "That was a first-place ride, all right."

"Slow though," Lauren pointed out. "And look, Jake's not backing all the way through the poles," she added.

Next Alicia, then Ginny, then a Manchester student took their turns. They did good jobs, but Jina had them beat. Finally, all of the riders had gone except Tommy.

Mary Beth crossed her fingers. She wanted Tommy to win. Not just because of her bet with Andie, but because she had called him Captain Wimpy. Jina's performance had been very good, though. Mary Beth didn't think he had a chance.

She studied Tommy. He sat easily on Lukas, patting the gray's neck. When Mrs. Caufield announced his name, he gathered his reins and urged the horse into a quiet trot.

Lukas trotted to the mailbox, his tail swishing uneasily. When Tommy opened the door, the horse was startled. But Tommy used his voice and legs to keep him from bolting.

Then Tommy turned Lukas toward the tarp and began to canter, something no one else had done. Lukas jumped the tarp, turned sharply, leaped over the crossbar, then switched directions and sailed over the plywood.

"Wow," Lauren gasped.

Mary Beth was speechless. Spellbound, she watched Tommy back Lukas between the two poles. Then the pair cantered to the finish line.

Loud applause broke out.

"Tommy had to have the fastest time," Mary Beth blurted. "That means the red team got first and I won the bet. Wait until I see Andie!"

"What do you win?" Lauren asked.

Mary Beth bit her lip. There was no way she was going to tell Lauren what Andie had said about Tommy liking her. It was too silly.

"Nothing," she said.

Mrs. Caufield checked her watch. "First place goes to Tommy Isaacson and the red team!" she announced. She walked over and pinned the blue ribbon on Lukas's bridle, and Tommy rode him from the ring.

Mary Beth couldn't wait to congratulate him.

"Wake up, Dan," she told the big horse. "We have to tell Tommy what a super job he did." Ignoring her, Dan flapped his lips sleepily and swished his tail at an imaginary fly. Mary Beth jiggled the reins. "Dan," she pleaded.

Lauren poked her in the ribs. "Mary Beth," she whispered urgently.

"What?" Mary Beth turned to look at her roommate. Lauren's blue eyes were as big as quarters.

"L-l-look over there!" Lauren stammered, jerking her head to the left.

Mary Beth craned her neck, trying to see what her roommate was staring at. A boy wearing trim-fitting, buff-colored breeches, high black boots, and a Manchester sweatshirt was walking toward the ring leading April Fool, one of Foxhall's horses. He was about as tall as Mary Beth, with brown hair.

"What? Where?" Mary Beth asked, not sure what Lauren was gaping at. "Are you talking about that guy leading April Fool?"

"Yes!" Lauren gasped, bobbing her head furiously. "That's him!"

"Who?" Mary Beth frowned, totally confused.

"The guy you were dancing with last night," Lauren exclaimed. She grabbed Mary Beth's wrist and squeezed it hard. "That guy is Zorro!"

9

Mary Beth stiffened. "Zorro?" she repeated in disbelief. She stared hard at the boy, trying to picture him dressed all in black with a cape and hat. "How can you tell?"

"Look at his boots!" Lauren hissed. "He's the only one wearing black boots. Did Zorro have hair that color?"

"I'm not sure." Mary Beth's heart began to race. The boy was the right height and build. And he was cute with curly, brown hair and broad shoulders. Definitely a seventh-grader.

Could it be him?

The boy stopped about ten feet in front of Mary Beth and Lauren and turned to check his girth. Mary Beth inhaled sharply.

Would he look at her? Would he recognize her? Would he smile or wave or—

Anything?

Mary Beth stood frozen. Another Manchester student came up to the boy in the sweatshirt and started talking to him. The boy in the sweatshirt turned to face Mary Beth. Lifting his head, he caught her eyes, just for an instant. Then he led April Fool away.

"He looked at you!" Lauren squealed. "It must be him!"

Blood rushed to Mary Beth's cheeks. "Then why didn't he come over and say hi?"

Lauren dug her fingers deeper into Mary Beth's wrist. "Maybe he's too shy. Maybe *you* need to say something to him first!"

Mary Beth shook her head. "No way. He ducked out on me last night. Remember?"

"Come on, Mary Beth," Lauren said. "You can't just do nothing."

"Oh, yes I can."

"Hey, what's up?" Andie sauntered toward them, thumbs hooked in her pockets. Jina was right behind her, leading Jake. "Besides the fact that the *red* team is winning so far," she boasted, giving Lauren and Jina superior looks.

Lauren ignored her. Grabbing Jina by the elbow, she spun her around. "Jina, look at that guy over there. The one holding April Fool.

Don't you think he looks like Zorro?"

"Lauren!" Mary Beth protested. "Would you cut it out?" She couldn't believe Lauren was making such a big deal out of this.

Squinting into the sun, Jina studied the brown-haired boy. "It might be." She grinned at Mary Beth. "Why don't you find out for sure?"

"How?" Mary Beth snapped. She was sick of hearing about Zorro. "Should I smell his boots to see if they have onion dip on them?"

Andie, Jina, and Lauren burst out laughing.

"What's so funny?" Tommy asked, walking up. His helmet was tucked under his arm, his hair plastered on his forehead.

"Nothing!" Mary Beth blurted, scowling at her roommates. If one of them told Tommy about last night, she'd kill her.

"Congratulations," she added quickly. "You did great in the obstacle race!"

He grinned. "Thanks."

"You were terrific, too, Jina," Lauren said.

"Well, if I'd been riding Superstar, I would have done better." Jina looked at Tommy. "Where'd you learn to jump like that?"

Tommy shrugged. "My dad's Ralph Isaac-son."

Andie's brows shot up. "Ralph Isaacson who rides Grand Prix jumpers?" she asked.

Tommy nodded.

Mary Beth looked at her roommates. She had no idea who Ralph Isaacson was, but from her roommates' excited expressions, she figured he must be a big deal.

"Well, I guess I can't call you Captain Wimpy anymore," Andie said, laughing.

Tommy grinned. "Oh, that's okay."

"Lauren, it's almost time for the pairs race," Jina said. "You'd better get Whisper."

"Oh, right!" Lauren whirled around and shook her finger in Mary Beth's face. "Now don't forget to go up to him," she said before she rushed off with Jina.

"Well, I'd better go give Alicia and Michael some advice," Andie said. "They're riding in the pairs, too. I don't want Jina and Lauren beating them."

Winking at Mary Beth, she mouthed, "Zorro." Then she ran off, too.

When her roommates were gone, Mary Beth breathed a sigh of relief and patted Dan on the neck. Then she stood on tiptoe and peeked over the saddle. Was the guy in the sweatshirt still there?

He was! Mounted on April, he sat straight and tall in the saddle. His boots gleamed in the sun, and his riding helmet was pulled low on his forehead. Mary Beth's heart skipped a beat. Seeing him in a hat made her realize he had to be the one. He was Zorro!

"What are you looking at?"

Mary Beth whirled around. She'd forgotten Tommy was still there.

"Oh, nothing," Mary Beth fibbed. "Do you think Michael and Alicia will win?"

"I don't know." He cracked his knuckles, then peered sideways at her. "So, are you going to the farewell dinner dance tonight?" he asked.

"Umm—" Mary Beth hesitated, her palms starting to sweat. Andie was right. Tommy *did* like her. "Yeah, I guess so. I mean, we have to go. I never pass up a chance to eat."

And to see Zorro, she added silently. She glanced over her shoulder. Would he be there? Would he come up to her then?

She watched him ride toward the ring with the other boy from Manchester. They must be in the pairs class, too, she decided.

Clucking to Dan, she hurried toward the rail. "Come on, Tommy," she said. "We have to see this race and cheer the red team on."

Six pairs of horses walked side by side around the ring, the riders holding the ends of a ribbon stretched between them. Mary Beth spotted Jina and Lauren.

Jake and Whisper walked perfectly abreast, their strides even. Alicia on Lukas and Michael, riding Windsor, another Foxhall horse, weren't doing as well. Lukas pranced ahead, while Windsor, an older horse, plodded along quietly. Alicia was having a hard time keeping hold of the ribbon.

"Uh-oh. I think the red team's in for trouble," Tommy said.

Mary Beth nodded, but her mind was on the boy mounted on April Fool. He and his partner kept their horses tightly reined as they tried to keep their paces even. They were on the green team.

"Trot!" Mrs. Caufield called through the bullhorn.

Mary Beth crossed her fingers. She wasn't sure who she wanted to win—her friends Jina and Lauren, her red team members, or Zorro and his partner.

Jina and Lauren trotted past, the ribbon taut between them. When Alicia and Michael came by, Lukas broke into a canter and the ribbon flew from Alicia's fingers.

Tommy groaned. "They're out of the race now. Sixth place. That's only one point for our team."

Mary Beth barely heard him. She was too busy watching Zorro. He was frowning intently, concentrating on keeping April next to his partner's horse, a bony ex-racehorse named T. L., which was short for Too Lazy to Race.

"Tommy, who's that Manchester guy who just went past on the chestnut mare?" Mary Beth asked.

"Jason Giroux," Tommy replied. "Why?"

Mary Beth shrugged. "I just think he's a good rider."

"He's an okay rider," Tommy said flatly.

Jason. Mary Beth whispered the name. It was a nice name.

She smiled to herself as she watched Jason and his partner canter past. Just then, the ribbon flew from Jason's fingers. He jerked April to a halt.

"Actually, if you ask me, he's kind of a rough rider," Tommy added.

I think he's a super rider, Mary Beth thought.

And she was going to tell Jason so, right after the pairs race.

Her heart pounding at her gutsy decision, Mary Beth was only dimly aware that Jina and Lauren had won the race. When the riders began leaving the ring, she handed Dan's reins to Tommy.

"Will you hold him a second?" she asked. Not waiting for Tommy's reply, she walked briskly toward April Fool and Jason.

She was going to do it. She was going to say something to him. But she knew she had to do it fast, before she chickened out.

His back was toward her as he ran up his stirrup irons.

"Hi," she said brightly. "You and April did a good job."

He glanced at her over his shoulder, his green eyes studying her. Mary Beth tried to remember the color of Zorro's eyes. Had they been green?

"April?" the guy repeated as he walked around April's head to the other side. "Is that the horse's name?"

"Uh, yeah." Mary Beth's mouth went dry and her hands felt clammy.

This isn't going right, she thought, starting to

panic. His eyes were supposed to light up when he saw who she was.

"Ashley Stewart usually rides her, only right now she's in the hospital," she rushed on stupidly, not knowing what else to say. "She's a really good show horse."

Jason grunted. "She didn't do too well in the pairs race."

"That's too bad." Mary Beth's smile died. She could see only the top of Jason's head as he secured the stirrup on the right side, but she could tell by the tone of his voice that he wasn't interested in talking to her.

Then it dawned on her—why he didn't want to talk to her now—or ever. He must have watched her ride in the egg race. He must have known right away that she was only a klutzy beginner.

What an idiot you are, Mary Beth silently scolded herself. *No wonder he's ignoring you— he's embarrassed to be seen with such a lousy rider.*

Without another word, Mary Beth spun around and raced blindly into the crowd of people and horses.

10

"Mary Beth? Are you in there?"

Mary Beth heard Jina, then Lauren call into Dan's stall, where she was huddled in the soft straw. Knees drawn up, her face in arms, she pretended she was a turtle hiding in its shell.

Go away, she wanted to tell them.

The latch clunked, the door creaked open, and straw rustled. Mary Beth didn't look up.

"Tommy said he saw you head this way," Lauren said. "We figured you might be in here."

"He said you were talking to some guy, and then you ran off," Jina added.

There was a long pause. Mary Beth imagined Lauren and Jina looking at each other, their brows raised, wondering what to do next.

Lauren cleared her throat. "We thought

Jason might be Zorro, and that when you went up to him he . . ." Her voice trailed off.

"Ignored me?" Mary Beth blurted, raising her head. "He did worse than that. He acted like I was some kind of freak."

"That's terrible!" Lauren said.

"And I felt like a freak, too," Mary Beth said. "Thanks, guys, for telling me I should go up to him first because maybe he was too *shy*." She buried her head back in her arms.

"How were we supposed to know he was a jerk?" Jina asked. "He was nice last night, right?"

"Right," Mary Beth mumbled. "Only I guess Zorro was the nice one." She sighed. "What a bonehead I am. To think some Manchester boy was going to like me."

"You're not a bonehead." Lauren plunked down in the straw next to her. "We've all liked guys who didn't like us back, right, Jina?"

"Uh, yeah," Jina stammered.

"Well, I have, anyway," Lauren continued. "Look at me and my crush on Todd."

"At least he talks to you," Mary Beth said glumly.

Lauren smiled at her. "Hey, at least all of this made you forget Brad."

Mary Beth groaned. "Dumped by two guys in one weekend."

Not that either was really my boyfriend, she added silently.

"That must be a world's record," Jina joked.

Even Mary Beth had to giggle at that.

"So, are you feeling better?" Lauren asked her.

Mary Beth grinned at her two roommates. "Yeah. Sorry I yelled at you guys."

"No problem," Jina said. She glanced out the stall door. "Hey, we'd better get back to the ring and get our horses. The team relay races are next."

"Oh, goody," Mary Beth muttered as she stood up. She followed Lauren and Jina out the door and down the drive. Tommy was heading toward them leading Dan, Whisper, Jake, and Lukas.

Mary Beth laughed. "He looks like a dog walker."

"You three had better hurry," Tommy said when the girls reached him. He handed Jake's reins to Jina and Whisper's reins to Lauren. "The red, green, and blue teams are racing first. Then the orange, yellow, and purple teams go. The winners of the two heats will compete against each other."

Reluctantly, Mary Beth took Dan's reins.

"Our team is over by the dressage arena," Tommy told her. "Jina and Lauren, your team's meeting under that big oak tree by the stable. We're racing in the big pasture."

"Thanks," Lauren said. She and Jina waved good-bye, then hurried to find their team.

Mary Beth and Tommy walked down to the dressage arena, their horses trailing slightly behind. Tommy glanced curiously at her, as if expecting her to say something. Mary Beth pressed her lips together.

There was no way she was going to tell Tommy about Jason and Zorro. All this boy stuff was too stupid.

"Is Andie psyched up to win?" Mary Beth asked, finally breaking the silence.

Tommy nodded. "She's driving Michael and Alicia crazy, making them practice passing the baton." He pointed to the arena.

Andie, Michael, and Alicia were mounted on their horses. Andie was trotting Ranger toward Michael and Windsor. A long wooden rod was in her right hand. She had her arm stretched out, ready to pass the baton to Michael. He had stuck his left arm behind him, ready to grab it from her.

When Andie was about five feet away, Michael signaled Windsor to trot. At the same time, he reached for the baton, grasped it firmly, and trotted toward Alicia. When he passed the baton to Alicia, she fumbled and dropped it.

Mary Beth grimaced. The relay race looked hard. All the team members were required to participate, so she couldn't get out of it. She hoped she didn't blow it. She'd already made a fool of herself today, even if she did win a blue ribbon.

"Hey, don't look so miserable," Tommy said when they stopped in front of the arena. "It's just a game. Need a leg up?" He came around to Dan's left side.

Mary Beth nodded. It was time for her to stop feeling sorry for herself. She tightened the girth and let down the stirrups. Ready to mount, she held on to the reins and Dan's withers with her left hand and the cantle with her right. Then she bent her right knee, lifting her lower leg at the same time.

Tommy stood by her left side. He placed his left hand under her bent knee and his right hand under her right foot.

"Okay. On the count of three," he said. "One, two, three."

Mary Beth jumped up as Tommy lifted. She flew halfway over the saddle, landing on her stomach with a hard smack.

"Oops, sorry. I didn't push you high enough," Tommy said. "Dan's so big."

"And I'm so heavy," Mary Beth said, laughing. She was draped over the saddle like a sack.

Tommy laughed, too.

Just then, Andie trotted up on Ranger, scowling. "Did you see Alicia drop the baton?" she said disgustedly, as she halted Ranger in front of Dan. "And she thought it was *funny*. I mean, the girl had better get serious. We're tied with the blue team. If we don't win this event, we're in major trouble."

Mary Beth just laughed louder. The blood was rushing to her face, and her unstrapped helmet was about to fall off.

"What's wrong with her?" Andie asked Tommy. "Why is she hanging there like that?"

"Uh, she's practicing for the next race," he said, straight-faced.

Mary Beth was laughing so hard, she started to snort. *If only Zorro could see me now,* she thought gleefully.

Andie sighed loudly in exasperation. Ranger chomped anxiously on his bit.

"How did I get on the same team with such losers?" she fumed. "Am I the only one who cares if we win or not?"

"Yes," Mary Beth gasped, struggling to pull herself into the saddle. Finally, she flung her right leg over the cantle and straightened.

Tommy mounted Lukas, jumping easily and lightly into the saddle.

"Show-off," Mary Beth told him. Tommy grinned back at her.

Andie rolled her eyes. "I can't believe you guys are so juvenile." Shading her face, she gazed toward the main ring. Mrs. Caufield was calling for the first three teams to ride out to the big pasture.

Michael and Alicia rode up from the arena.

"Are we ready?" Michael asked. His cowboy hat and boots were covered with dust.

"Well, *I* am," Andie said. "Tommy, why don't you and Lukas race first to give the team a head start? You can pass the baton to Michael. Ranger and I will go last to make up for any lost time."

"Michael can pass the baton to me," Alicia

93

said, still giggling. "Since we're so good at it."

Andie just glared at her.

Mary Beth stuck her feet in the stirrups, strapped on her helmet, and gathered her reins. Dan had fallen asleep while she was mounting. He was probably sick of these games, too. She swatted him on the butt, trying to get his attention.

"Mary Beth, you go. . . " Andie hesitated ". . . next to last. You'll pass the baton to me." She moved Ranger right beside Dan. "So don't blow it," she added in a threatening voice.

Mary Beth saluted sharply. She wasn't going to let Andie get to her. Tommy was right. It was just a game.

The group rode up the hill with the other teams and through the gate into the pasture. The field was fairly flat and had been recently mowed. Red, blue, and green flags with numbers on them marked the course for each team.

Everyone gathered around Mrs. Caufield while she explained the rules. "Each horse and rider trots to his or her team's colored flag, where the next rider will be waiting. If you drop the baton during a pass, you may jump off, remount, and pass it again," she said

"Only the last rider is allowed to canter to the finish line."

"Canter?" Andie whispered to Mary Beth. "Ranger and I are going to gallop!"

"Is everyone ready?" Mrs. Caufield asked.

"Yes!" the riders chorused.

Mary Beth frowned. All she had to do was trot Dan in a straight line and hand the baton to Andie.

She could handle that.

Tommy halted Lukas at the starting line and wished his teammates good luck. Mary Beth followed Andie down the row of red flags. Michael stopped by flag 1, and Alicia stopped at flag 2. Mary Beth went straight to flag 3.

Andie gave her a warning look. "Don't drop that baton, Finney, or I'll make you eat it."

"Want to make another bet, Perez?" Mary Beth shot back as Andie rode up to flag 4. "You lost the last one, remember?" she called after her.

Mary Beth saw Lauren by the second blue flag, and waved. Jina was ahead at flag 4 with Andie. They'd be racing each other to the finish line.

Mary Beth glanced around, wondering who

she'd be racing against. She caught her breath. Mounted on April Fool by the green flag 3 was Zorro!

His head was turned away from her, as he watched the riders at the starting line. Mary Beth gulped, and beads of sweat began to drip from under her helmet.

"Are all riders ready?" Dr. Kresky shouted through the bullhorn. Manchester's headmaster was positioned at the starting gate, a starter's gun in his hand. Mrs. Caufield stood at the finish line.

Forget about Zorro, Mary Beth told herself. She twisted in the saddle, trying to find Tommy. He was leaning forward, his reins tight as Lukas pranced sideways. When the gun went off, Lukas leaped in the air.

Tommy pulled him around. Hooves flying, Lukas trotted toward Michael.

Goose bumps of excitement raced up Mary Beth's arms. She glanced at Zorro. When the gun went off, April had spun in a circle.

Maybe I'll beat him, Mary Beth thought as she watched him roughly steer April next to the flag. She bit back a smile. *That would show him.*

Suddenly, a shout behind her made her

jump. Alicia was already trotting toward her, the baton raised like a knight's lance.

Mary Beth inhaled sharply. "Dan! Get ready!" She flapped the reins, trying to get the horse's attention. Then she swiveled in the saddle, ready to grab the baton.

Alicia trotted up on her horse and slapped the baton into Mary Beth's hand. When Mary Beth's fingers closed tight around the rod, she breathed a sigh of relief.

"Go, Dan!" She nudged him hard with her legs.

He grunted and walked two steps. Mary Beth kicked him harder. His walk quickened, but not much. She couldn't believe this was happening to her. She'd forgotten her whip, and Dan wouldn't trot!

"Dan!" she screeched.

Zorro and April flew past. Ahead of her, Andie was waving wildly, her face beet red. Frantically, Mary Beth pummeled Dan with her heels. His walk turned into a jog, but Zorro and the rider from the blue team had already reached flag 4.

The blood drained from Mary Beth's cheeks. They were going to lose the race, and it was all her fault!

11

As she and Dan trotted toward Andie, Mary Beth caught a glimpse of her roommate's face. Andie was glaring daggers at her. Her lips were pressed together so hard they were white. The other riders were already cantering toward the finish line.

Mary Beth swallowed hard. She wanted to turn Dan around and trot in the other direction. Anywhere so she didn't have to face Andie.

As Dan reached Ranger, Andie's nostrils flared—like a bull ready to charge.

"I'm sorry," Mary Beth said. "I couldn't get him to trot."

Andie didn't say a word. Without taking the baton from Mary Beth, she cantered the big horse toward the finish line.

Tears filled Mary Beth's eyes. *It's only a game,* she wanted to shout after Andie. But she knew how much Andie wanted to win.

Dumb move, Finney. Mary Beth wiped her cheeks on her jacket sleeve. She'd been so worried about Zorro she hadn't paid attention to the race. She'd blown it.

"Hey, are you okay?" Tommy trotted up on Lukas.

Mary Beth nodded. "Sure. It's just a game, right?"

He didn't say anything, either.

He's mad, too. Not that Mary Beth blamed him. Right now, she could hear Mrs. Caufield announcing that the blue team were the winners of the relay race. That meant they'd probably won the competition for the day, too. Mary Beth sighed. At least Jina and Lauren would be happy.

When Tommy still didn't reply, Mary Beth spun around in the saddle to face him.

"Why don't you say it?" she demanded. "Why don't you just tell me that it was all my fault that we lost?"

Startled, Tommy's brows shot up.

"So I'm a lousy rider and I should never have been competing," she continued. Her voice kept rising, even though she knew there was no reason to yell at him. "I should have been cleaning up the smashed eggs after the egg race!"

"Cleaning up the eggs?" Tommy repeated. He looked at her, confused, then he started to laugh. "That's pretty funny."

"It is not," Mary Beth said darkly. Just then, Dan pulled his head down and grabbed a clump of grass. Exasperated, Mary Beth let him take a few bites before pulling hard on the reins.

"You're not a lousy rider," Tommy said.

"Oh, give me a break." Mary Beth swung her right leg over the back of the saddle, and dismounted. She'd had enough. "Admit it, Tommy. You're just as mad as everyone else on the team."

Tommy shrugged. "I really did think it was funny. Kind of like last night when you dropped that dip on my—" He stopped abruptly, as if suddenly realizing he'd made a mistake.

Mary Beth snapped her chin up. "That was *you*?"

"Um—" he stammered. His gaze darted from Mary Beth to the ground, and his neck slowly turned pink. Finally, he nodded, a pained expression on his face. "Yeah."

Mary Beth stared at him. *Tommy was Zorro?*

She didn't know what to say, what to think. All this time she'd thought Jason was the mysterious Zorro. No wonder he'd looked at her so strangely when she'd started talking to him.

"Why didn't you tell me?" she asked. "Why'd you let me make a fool of myself in front of Jason and all of my roommates?"

Suddenly, Mary Beth realized how furious she was about the whole thing. "And why did you run out on me last night?" she practically shouted.

Tommy's neck grew even redder. He opened his mouth as if to say something, but no words came out. Mary Beth's fingers tightened on the reins. "And all this time I thought you were my friend," she said. "Come on, Dan. We're finished for the day. Let's get you untacked."

Turning her back on Tommy, Mary Beth marched across the pasture, leading Dan. She couldn't hold back the tears any longer.

This is just like what happened with Brad, she thought, tears rolling down her cheeks. Tommy and Brad were both supposed to be her friends. And they'd both betrayed her. Mary Beth couldn't believe how much it hurt.

"How does this look?" Lauren held up a corduroy jumper and flowered print turtleneck. The four roommates were back in the suite, getting ready for the farewell dinner dance.

"It looks like an outfit you wore when you were still in diapers," Andie said. She was leaning over her dresser, staring into the mirror as she brushed on mascara. She wore a red sweater over a black miniskirt with red leggings and black lace-up boots.

Lauren's face fell. "Oh." With a sigh, she turned back to the open wardrobe.

Mary Beth was already dressed. Not that she cared what she wore. Sitting in her desk chair, she hunched over a book, pretending to read. She hadn't told her roommates about Tommy being Zorro. And she wasn't going to, either.

She didn't want to hear their nosy questions, their teasing, their unhelpful comments. She just wanted the whole horrible weekend to be over.

Jina stood in the bathroom doorway, toweldrying her hair. "Take a look at some of my skirts, Lauren," she suggested. "I've got an ultrasuede one that might fit you. It has a matching vest."

"That sounds neat." Lauren started sorting through the clothes in the wardrobe. "So what do you guys think about the haunted ride we're going on tonight? Doesn't it sound fun?"

Mary Beth looked up from her book. "What haunted ride?"

Andie stopped applying mascara to look at her. "Oh, that's right, Finney. You left the games *early* and didn't hear the big news."

Mary Beth ignored the sarcastic tone in Andie's voice. Jina sat down on Mary Beth's bed to comb out her wet hair.

"This morning, before the games, the girls in the Horsemasters Club fixed up one of the trails with ghosts and scary stuff," Jina explained. "After dinner, everyone's riding the trail, either on horseback or in a hay wagon."

"Oh," Mary Beth said flatly. Any other time, she would have thought it was a great idea. Tonight, she thought it stunk.

"Chad wants me to ride in the wagon with him," Lauren said, giggling.

"Oh, how *sweet*," Andie said.

"Maybe I'll go in the wagon, too," Mary

Beth said. Then she wouldn't have to see Tommy.

"Sorry," Jina said. "Caufield said there's not much room in the wagon. All the students in the riding program have to ride horses."

"Too bad, Lauren. No holding hands with Chaddiepoo," Andie teased.

Lauren ignored her. She'd slipped on Jina's tan skirt and vest, pairing it with her turtleneck. "So how's *this*?"

"Better," Andie said.

"It looks great." Jina jumped off the bed and pulled a drop-waisted, flower-print dress from the wardrobe. "And now *I'd* better get moving."

Soon, all the roommates were ready for dinner. Mary Beth had to admit they looked good. Usually, none of them wore makeup. But tonight, even Jina had put on blush and a touch of mascara. *Not that she needs it with her already-perfect dark lashes,* Mary Beth thought.

"Hey, do we look sharp or what?" Andie asked. "Except for Finney, of course."

Mary Beth had decided just to wear her navy blue skirt and Foxhall blazer.

"I guess she already got enough attention

today," Andie went on, glaring meaningfully at Mary Beth.

"Oh, shut up, Andie," Lauren said. "She won the egg race. And Ranger took first in the school race. What more did you want?"

"Hmmph." Andie didn't reply. Instead she fluffed her already-full hair and stalked out the door.

The four girls trooped into the hallway. It was already filled with giggling girls, ready to join the Manchester boys for dinner.

When they reached the courtyard outside the dorm, Jina and Andie hurried ahead. Lauren fell in beside Mary Beth.

"You're awfully quiet," she said. "Is everything all right?"

Mary Beth nodded. "Sure. I'm just tired."

"You're not really upset about the relay race, are you? I mean, you weren't the only one who goofed. Ginny and Shandra dropped their batons. And some guy almost fell off Shakespeare."

"No, it's not the games," Mary Beth reassured her friend.

Lauren snapped her fingers as they climbed the steps to the dining hall. "I know what's bothering you. It's that Jason guy."

"No, really, it's nothing," Mary Beth said.

She opened the door into the dining room, and Lauren followed her inside. The large room was packed with teachers and students from both schools. Mary Beth looked straight ahead as she and Lauren were directed to different tables. Name cards were placed in front of each glass. Mary Beth was seated between a Manchester junior named Joey and a seventh-grader named Hal.

She unfolded her napkin on her lap. Hal and Joey were talking about the soccer game. It sounded really boring.

Mary Beth looked around at the other kids around the table. She didn't recognize any of them. With a sigh of relief, she sipped her water. She hoped no one would recognize her from the riding games.

Dinner was being served by Foxhall's Junior Service Club. A girl wearing a big smile and a Foxhall blazer placed a plate of steaming roast beef, beans almondine, and new potatoes in front of Mary Beth.

The meal smelled yummy, but for once Mary Beth didn't feel like eating. Slowly, she picked up her fork and speared a bean. As she stuck it in her mouth, she noticed Tommy sitting two tables away. Tiffany Dubray, another sixth-grader, sat next to him. Tiffany was bobbing her blond head as she talked his ear off. Tommy was listening earnestly.

Mary Beth swallowed the bean whole. It caught in her throat. Picking up her glass, she gulped down her water, spilling drops on her blouse.

Joey turned to stare at her. She tried to smile as she wiped the dribbles off her chin.

Way to go, Finney, she congratulated herself.

Actually, it *was* pretty funny, she thought, biting back a grin. Kind of like spilling onion dip on Zorro's boot. She laughed out loud.

Hal, the seventh-grader, looked at her suspiciously. She grinned at him, knowing that a bean was probably caught between her teeth. Disgusted, he looked quickly away. Mary Beth happily smeared butter on her potatoes. *It's time to quit moping,* she told herself. *No guy is worth all this trouble.* As she sliced her beef, her mouth began to water.

Dinner looked delicious, she decided. She was going to enjoy every bite.

12

"Tommy's staring at you again, Mary Beth," Lauren said, as she rode beside her on Whisper. Mary Beth was plodding along on Dan. "He keeps turning around in the saddle."

"So?" Mary Beth said, shrugging. It was a beautiful evening for the trail ride. It wasn't too cold, even for late October, and there were a zillion stars in the sky.

Mary Beth looked straight ahead, determined not to notice Tommy. Luckily for her, Dan had fallen behind the group of students and horses strung in a line as they walked up an old logging road and into a field. Following the horses, Dorothy drove a tractor which pulled a wagon stacked with straw bales. Mary Beth could hear the students and teachers on the wagon singing.

"What is *with* you, Mary Beth?" Lauren asked. Halting Whisper, she waited for Dan to catch up. "Don't you even care? I mean, it's so obvious that Tommy likes you."

"Then why did he dance with Tiffany after dinner?" Mary Beth said sulkily.

"Because you kept ducking into the bathroom," Lauren said. "Then you disappeared like Cinderella."

"I didn't disappear. I just went back to the suite for a while," Mary Beth retorted.

"You're impossible," Lauren said.

Mary Beth heard the roar of the tractor coming up right behind them. She squeezed her left leg into Dan's side and steered him into the field. The tractor chugged past.

A boy sitting on the wagon waved to Lauren. Smiling, she waved back.

"Who is that?" Mary Beth asked.

"Frank," Lauren said.

"What happened to Chad?"

Lauren shrugged. Frank beckoned to Lauren to follow them. Whisper eyed the noisy wagon as Lauren rode her closer.

Mary Beth waited until it had gone past before asking Dan to walk. Tiffany Dubray was sitting on the back on the wagon, her legs dangling casually over the side.

"Your horse is kind of slow, Mary Beth," Tiffany called over the roar of the tractor.

"And your mouth is kind of big," Mary Beth murmured under her breath.

"Maybe you both need a ride on the wagon," Tiffany added, giggling.

Mary Beth pretended she didn't hear her.

As they crossed the field, Dan fell farther behind. Up ahead was the haunted woods. Mary Beth figured she'd catch up with the others there.

As the tractor reached the woods, Mary Beth noticed a horse and rider waiting for her. It was Lukas and Tommy.

"Hi," he said after the tractor rumbled past.

"Hi," Mary Beth said brightly, trying to sound normal. She wasn't going to show him how hurt she was.

Lukas spun on his hind legs, eager to catch up with the other horses. Collecting him lightly, Tommy swung the gray next to Dan. Mary Beth thought he was one of the most natural riders she'd ever seen.

"Whoa, Lukas, easy," Tommy said, patting him. The two horses touched noses.

"You don't have to ride back here with me," Mary Beth said.

"I want to. I mean, I didn't get to talk to you at dinner."

"Oh? Well, I guess I didn't see you."

Tommy cocked his head. "Yes, you did. You just didn't want to talk to me."

"That's not true," Mary Beth protested.

"You're still mad because I ducked out on you at the Halloween dance."

Abruptly, Mary Beth reached down and laced her fingers through Dan's coarse mane. They walked past two pumpkins on a hay bale. A sign propped against the pumpkins read, HAUNTED WOODS—BEWARE! Bobbing at different points along the trail were colorful lanterns to light the way.

"I don't blame you," Tommy continued. "I was a jerk to leave. I guess I just panicked."

"Panicked?" Mary Beth repeated, puzzled. They passed two witches stirring a pot of brew. The witches, who looked suspiciously like Foxhall teachers, cackled. Lukas snorted and jigged sideways.

"Well, I—I—" Tommy began. "This is going to sound so stupid."

Mary Beth pretended to be fascinated with a tree limb bobbing with bats.

"I mean, before we got to Foxhall," Tommy explained, "the upperclass guys told us no Foxhall girls would ever dance with us geeky sixth-graders."

Mary Beth couldn't help but be interested in what Tommy was saying. Still, she stared intently at a Frankenstein mask in a tree so she wouldn't look *too* interested.

"But when I got to the dance, the music was pretty good, and I felt different. You know, as if the Zorro costume made me someone else." He cleared his throat. "And then I met you and I thought, well, why not?"

Lukas snorted at a straw-stuffed body lying by the side of the trail. Dan eyed it lazily.

"So I came over, winning you over with great conversation, and you asked me to dance."

"Great conversation? As I remember, you asked me not to eat all the dip," Mary Beth said.

Tommy grinned. "And then you dropped it on my boot. Hey, Lukas, cut it out!" He short-ened his reins as the gray shied from a gooey, red blob alongside the trail.

"What's that?" Tommy asked.

Mary Beth wrinkled her nose. "I think it's supposed to be some dead thing. Only it looks more like the cafeteria's spaghetti and meatballs."

Tommy laughed.

"Okay, so after you won me over with your wit, what happened next?" Mary Beth urged.

"Well, I was really having a good time." Tommy smiled shyly at her in the darkness. Mary Beth smiled back, then ducked her chin, suddenly embarrassed.

"But then I told that stupid lie about being a seventh-grader. I only did it because of what the other guys had said. Then your headmaster announced it was time to take off our masks, and I was afraid you'd guess I was only a wimpy sixth-grader. So I hid in the bus until it was time to go."

"Why didn't you say something this afternoon?" Mary Beth asked.

"I wanted to. But then Andie called me a wimpy sixth-grader, and I figured that's what you saw me as, too."

"And then I thought Jason was Zorro," Mary Beth said with a sigh. "What a dope I was."

The two of them fell silent. A tape-recorded wolf howled, and someone laughed eerily. Then the wind whistled through the trees, sending several white, plastic-bag ghosts twirling. Lukas tossed his head nervously, as the tractor disappeared around a bend in the trail.

Mary Beth thought about what Tommy had said. It made her feel a lot better. Still, Tommy was such a good rider. He was used to hanging out with girls like Jina who competed at A-level shows—not girls like her who could barely ride.

"Listen, Mary Beth," Tommy began.

Mary Beth tensed, wondering what he was going to say.

"I'd really like to call you once in a while."

Mary Beth's mouth dropped open. "You're kidding."

"Why would I kid about that?"

"Because—because you're such a good rider. I mean, you must have noticed I was the worst rider at Foxhall. Everyone else did. I really blew the relay race."

"What does that have to do with calling you?"

"I don't know," Mary Beth said, shrugging.

"I just have a feeling it does."

She shivered in the cool night breeze as she and Tommy walked their horses silently along the dark trail. Suddenly, the wind whipped through the trees, sending a plastic-bag ghost flying from a limb. The ghost hit Lukas on the flank, startling the already-nervous horse.

He reared sharply, throwing his rider backward, and the reins flew from Tommy's hands. Tommy grabbed for the pommel as Lukas wheeled around, crashing into Dan's side.

Mary Beth was jolted forward. Dan planted his feet as Lukas scrambled against him, trying to get away from the ghost that had fallen on the path under his hooves.

"Lukas, whoa!" Tommy commanded, his voice steady. He was holding on to the pommel with both hands, to keep from falling off the careening horse.

Head high, nostrils flared, Lukas paused just long enough for Mary Beth to bend down and snatch up the reins. Suddenly, the gray bolted forward, his instinct telling him to run.

Desperately, Mary Beth held on tight.

If she let go, Lukas would run off. And without reins, Tommy wouldn't be able to stop his horse!

13

It felt as though Mary Beth held onto Lukas's reins forever. Finally, the bit caught Lukas in the mouth, yanking his head around. Dan stood firm.

Tommy finally regained his balance. Leaning forward, he took the reins from Mary Beth.

"Easy, Lukas," he crooned as he shortened his hold. Using his voice and legs, he turned Lukas in a circle and let him see the ghost. "It's just a white bag, you dummy."

The gray horse trembled. Arching his neck, he lowered his head and cautiously smelled the ghost. Mary Beth let out her breath. "That was a close one." Bending down, she gave Dan a pat. "Good job, buddy."

Dan just yawned. Mary Beth laughed, leaning over the pommel, and flung her arms around his huge neck.

Maybe Dan was slow, and maybe he had blown the relay race. But he had just proved he was the best horse in the world.

"Good job to *both* of you," Tommy said, after he had caught his breath. "I can't believe I lost my reins like that. It's never happened before. Ever." He gazed up the dark trail. The tractor had disappeared, though Mary Beth could still hear it. "I'm sure glad no one else noticed. You won't tell anyone what happened, will you? I mean, you were really brave and all, but . . ."

"I won't," Mary Beth promised. "We both might get in big trouble. We got separated from everyone, and neither of us was paying attention."

"I wasn't thinking of that." Tommy frowned. "I just don't want anyone to find out that the *worst* rider at Foxhall had to save *me* from getting dumped."

"Worst rider?" Mary Beth snapped. "Well, thanks a bunch!"

"Got you!" Tommy said. He burst out laughing, and Mary Beth realized he was only teasing.

He really doesn't care whether I'm a good rider,

she thought happily. *He likes me for me.*

"You know what, Tommy?" she said, suddenly feeling great. And why not? She and Dan *had* saved Tommy. Maybe the haunted woods weren't so haunted after all. "I'd really like it if you called me sometime."

"*Tommy* was Zorro?" Lauren exclaimed in disbelief.

Mary Beth nodded. She was unsaddling Dan after the trail ride. Lauren and Whisper stood in front of the stall door. Whisper, a wool cooler draped across her back, hung her head over the Dutch door while Lauren leaned on it.

"I can't believe it." Lauren shook her head. "Did you get to say good-bye to him?"

"Yeah. The Manchester bus just left. We were the last to come in from the trail ride, so Tommy had to hustle and untack Lukas."

Mary Beth pulled the saddle and pad off Dan. She'd told Lauren everything. Well, almost everything. She wasn't telling anyone about Lukas almost running away. The near-accident was her and Tommy's secret.

"Did you get to say good-bye to Chad? Or was it Frank?" Mary Beth teased Lauren as she set the saddle on the stall door.

Lauren grinned. "Both."

"You're as bad as Andie," Mary Beth told her.

"Hi, guys." Jina squeezed beside Whisper and Lauren. "Wasn't that a fun ride?"

"Yeah," Mary Beth said dreamily.

Jina looked questioningly at Lauren. "What's with her?"

Lauren told Jina all about Tommy being Zorro.

"That's so cool!" Jina said.

"And you know what else?" Mary Beth asked. She unbuckled the throatlatch on the bridle and turned to look at her two friends. "He's going to call me sometime this week."

Jina and Lauren squealed happily.

"Hey, what's all that squealing?" Andie asked. She stuck her head into the stall. Whisper backed up, moving into the aisle. "Is there a pig-calling contest going on in here?"

"Mary Beth's got a boyfriend!" Jina told her.

Andie looked doubtful. "No way. Not *Finney*."

"Tommy's not really a boyfriend," Mary Beth said quickly. She wasn't going to make the same mistake she had with Brad. "We just

119

had fun together this weekend."

"*Sure!*" Jina and Lauren chorused.

Mary Beth slipped the headpiece of the bridle over Dan's ears. The big horse opened his mouth and she eased the bit from between his teeth.

"Well, I'm glad *you* had fun this weekend," Andie said. "I thought the Manchester guys were all nerds."

"*Sure!*" Jina and Lauren chorused again, then burst out laughing.

"Really," Andie insisted, "I'm much more excited about next Saturday. My dad's coming for Parents' Weekend. He's going to watch me ride Magic."

Mary Beth picked up a brush from the grooming bucket. Dan wasn't sweaty, so she just needed to give him a good cleaning.

"I didn't know you were riding Magic yet," Jina said.

"Tomorrow." Andie's eyes lit up. "I'm so excited. I want my dad to see how well Magic's doing when he comes next weekend."

"Is your mom coming, Jina?" Lauren asked.

Jina nodded, though she didn't look too excited about the idea.

"And my parents just wrote that they're

coming, too!" Lauren said happily.

"Hey, Finney, that reminds me." Andie pulled an envelope out of her jacket pocket. "This came in the mail this morning."

Mary Beth stared at the letter. "This morning? Why didn't you give it to me then?"

Andie shrugged. "I was planning to. I guess I just forgot in all the excitement." She winked at Mary Beth. "It smells like cow manure, so I guess it must be from Brad."

"Brad?" Mary Beth hesitated, then slowly took the letter. Andie was right. It *was* from Brad. She recognized the return address.

What does he want? she wondered. He was probably going to tell her all about Emily Zentz. Maybe she should throw it away without reading it.

"Well?" Lauren said, her eyes wide. "Open it!"

Mary Beth looked up at her roommates. All three were leaning over the stall door, as if they were dying of curiosity. Even Dan turned his big head to sniff the envelope.

"Okay, okay." Mary Beth took a deep breath as she tore open the top and pulled out a piece of notebook paper. *It couldn't be worse news than what Janie had already written,* she told herself glumly.

Slowly, she unfolded it.

"Read it!" Andie insisted.

Mary Beth licked her lips, then started to read aloud.

"Dear Mary Beth,

Your friend Janie is crazy. She told me what she told you about me going out with Emily Zentz. WELL, IT'S NOT TRUE. Emily talks too much. I can't come next weekend because the Boy Scout Jamboree was switched because it rained last Saturday. Believe me, I'd much rather come to your school for Parents' Weekend. I have to share a tent with Danny Berkowitz and he snores. Maybe I'll see you when you come home for Thanksgiving.

Your friend,
Brad."

"He's a Boy Scout?" Andie sounded disgusted.

"Mary Beth, he still likes you!" Lauren exclaimed. "He's not going out with that Emily person. That's so great."

Mary Beth couldn't believe it. She'd spent

half the weekend worrying about Brad. If only she'd gotten the letter sooner.

"Andie, I should kill you for not giving this to me," she said, flapping the letter in Andie's face.

"Sorry-y-y," Andie said. She didn't look sorry at all.

"Hey, everything worked out okay, didn't it?" Jina reminded Mary Beth.

Still frowning, Mary Beth tucked the letter back in the envelope and stuck it in her jeans pocket. Then her frown softened. Jina was right. Everything *had* turned out okay.

Mary Beth grinned at her roommates. "Maybe it was a good thing Andie forgot to give the letter to me."

Andie raised one brow. "It was?"

"That's right!" Lauren said, catching on. "If you knew Brad still liked you, you might not have met Zorro."

"You mean Tommy," Jina corrected.

"Hey, I did good, didn't I?" Andie said, in a pleased voice.

Mary Beth whisked a brushful of dust in her direction. "Just don't do it again," she warned.

But inside she was really happy. Brad was

going to see her at Thanksgiving, Tommy had promised to call her, and she'd found out maybe she wasn't such a bad rider after all.

The weekend hadn't turned out half bad!

"Wow," Lauren said. "Mary Beth has two boyfriends."

"Just *friends*," Mary Beth said.

"But they're *boy* friends," Jina added, giggling.

"Finney with two guys?" Andie shook her head. "Miracles really do happen," she said.

For once, Mary Beth had to agree.

**Don't miss the next book
in the Riding Academy series:
#6: ANDIE SHOWS OFF**

"I hope Magic does okay when your dad comes for Parents' Weekend," Mary Beth said, her voice doubtful. "That horse is pretty crazy."

"He is not," Andie said sharply. "He's going to do great this weekend, and my dad will buy him for me. You just wait."

She flopped over on her bed, turning her back on Mary Beth. But her stomach was tightening into a knot.

What if Mary Beth was right?

The beautiful Thoroughbred had been doing so well. But she hadn't actually gotten to ride him yet. She had no idea how Magic would behave once she got on him.

Then another fear hit her. What if her father didn't come for Parents' Weekend? Her dad had broken promises before.

But this time he won't, Andie told herself, punching her pillow fiercely. *This time he'll come, and Magic will be perfect, and Dad will agree that he should be my horse.*

She hoped.

If you love horses, you'll enjoy these other Bullseye books:

THE BLACK STALLION
THE BLACK STALLION RETURNS
THE BLACK STALLION AND THE GIRL
SON OF THE BLACK STALLION
A SUMMER OF HORSES
WHINNY OF THE WILD HORSES